SEX WITH A STRANGER

SEX WITH A STRANGER

KATHERINE GARBERA

BRAVA

KENSINGTON PUBLISHING CORP.

http://www.kensingtonbooks.com

BRAVA BOOKS are published by

Kensington Publishing Corp.
850 Third Avenue
New York, NY 10022

All Kensington titles, imprints and distributed lines are available at special quantity discounts for bulk purchases for sales promotion, premiums, fund-raising, educational or institutional use.

Special book excerpts or customized printings can also be created to fit specific needs. For details, write or phone the office of the Kensington Special Sales Manager: Kensington Publishing Corp., 850 Third Avenue, New York, NY 10022. Attn. Special Sales Department. Phone: 1-800-221-2647.

Brava and the B logo Reg. U.S. Pat. & TM Off.

ISBN-13: 978-0-7582-2229-9
ISBN-10: 0-7582-2229-7

First Kensington Trade Paperback Printing: September 2007
10 9 8 7 6 5 4 3 2 1

Printed in the United States of America

SEX WITH A STRANGER

Prologue

He felt small and inconsequential, sitting alone in the dark in a run-down room on an unoccupied floor of the C&H Casino Hotel. He knew without a doubt that if he were to disappear tonight, no one would care or come looking for him.

That hadn't always been true. At one time he'd been a player in Vegas, but now he'd been reduced to this. A has-been. A footnote in someone else's story. He lit a cigarette, rubbing his hand over his scalp and searching . . .

The flame on the end of the cigarette burned clean and true and the more heavily he puffed, the brighter the flame got. He quickly finished his cigarette and lit another one. This time he barely noticed the soothing effect of the nicotine. Instead he concentrated on that small bit of flamey ash on the end. The way that it burned by his design, under his control.

He looked around the dingy room that smelled heavily of smoke. This hotel was old and run-down, not at all like the shiny, newer Royal Banner that was closer to the heart of the Vegas Strip.

Control—wasn't that what everyone said he lacked? He eyed the flame and then the bedspread.

It was an old print that he doubted had ever been eye-catching, one he knew was destined to be tossed out like trash. He took the spread off the bed and put it in the bathtub.

He scrubbed a hand over his face—what the hell was he doing?

Whatever the hell he wanted. No one gave a fuck if he lived or died, and it wasn't like he was hurting anyone.

Hell, it wasn't like anyone even knew he was here. The owner of the hotel preferred that he stayed away from this property.

He took out his lucky lighter—damn piece of crap hadn't exactly helped him at the tables lately—and leaned down. He flicked the igniter and watched the flame grow. He adjusted the length of the flame and flicked it again and the flame jumped even higher, almost singeing the hair on his arm.

Bending down, he touched the flame to the bedspread. That old bed linen burned quickly, the flames larger than he'd expected. He stared at them, watching them grow until they started licking at the wall behind the tub. But the tile wouldn't burn.

He blew on the fire and watched the flame change direction. It was hungry, the fire was, and it was looking for something else to consume. He used a towel to fan it, directing the flames toward the other end of the tub where there wasn't tile, just some ugly, fading wallpaper.

The flames liked the wallpaper, slowly moving up the wall and spreading toward the door.

He left the bathroom one step ahead of the flames. They were really burning now. He thought about closing the door, trapping the flames in there, but he wasn't finished playing with the fire yet.

It made him feel powerful to have something so destructive under his control. All he had to do was step outside and go down the hall, pull the fire alarm, and the fire would go out.

Fire was so much easier to control than life.

A breeze from the open balcony window stirred into the room just as the first bit of the flames licked around the corner of the wall. That breeze forced the flames higher and made them move quicker than he'd anticipated, blocking the only exit to the room.

A sense of panic enveloped him and he backed toward the balcony, climbing out onto it. The room next to his was completely dark. Supposedly empty. Hell, his room was considered empty by the hotel staff as well. It was only the fact that he'd known how to work the key card system downstairs that had enabled him to get into the room.

He threw his leg over the side of the rusted, wrought iron fencing on the balcony and reached out to steady himself on the one next door. He quickly climbed over into the neighboring room. He pushed hard on the slider, popping the lock and quickly entering the room.

He walked straight through, smelling the smoke. This time it wasn't the cigarette scent that had lingered for more than twenty years. This time it was the fresh scent coming off the new flames.

He opened the door to the hallway, saw the smoke sneaking out from under the door, and smiled to himself. He used his key card to open the door to the room. The flames roared and moaned as fresh air fed it, and he dropped his key card, running down the hall away from the flames. Standing at the entrance to the fire-escape stairs, he watched the blaze burn for as long as he could before the smoke alarm was activated and the sprinklers came on, slowing the progress of the flames. But not stopping it.

He ran down the stairs and out into the night. Next time he had to find a way to disable the sprinklers.

Chapter 1

Disabling the sprinklers had taken him longer than he'd ever anticipated. He'd set two other fires since that first one, but those other blazes had been for practice; to be honest, it was the Royal Banner that intrigued him. It had taken a few days for him to get access to the secured area that housed all of the security-alarm connections.

He knew how to disable alarms from his time living at home. He'd been locked out more than once during his "wild" days, whatever the hell that meant. He liked to have fun, but what the hell, that wasn't what tonight was about.

He'd disabled the alarm on the unoccupied floor of the hotel. The alarm and security camera systems were connected and it had taken longer than he would have liked to knock both of them out.

He knew it was only a matter of time, probably thirty minutes, before the security team got a call from the alarm center saying that the system was down. The only reason he even had that small window was due to all the construction taking place on the floor. They'd been intermittently turning the alarms off while the construction crew was working up there.

He took the stairs two at time. He liked the way that first bedspread had burned, but there weren't linens on any of the new mattresses yet, so he'd had to improvise.

Carrying a loose set of rags in a backpack, he entered a room in the far corner. The electronic locks had been disengaged when he'd turned off the security and fire alarms on this floor. He cut a hole in the mattress and then went to work.

Shoving the old rags into the hole he'd made, he pushed down on the igniter and watched the flame dancing for a minute, stirred by his breath. Then he bent down and touched it to the mattress.

There must have been some flame retardant on the mattress because the flames quickly died. Fuck that, he thought. He'd worked too hard to make this situation prime—no way was he going to just walk away.

He bent down and touched the lighter to the carpet underneath the bed and the flames started to spread. They moved slowly at first, and he sank down on the floor in the corner watching them burn. Watching them move slowly around the mattress and across the floor.

He knew he wasn't going to be able to make it to the door, but this time he was prepared. He took out the bowie knife his brother had given him when he was fourteen and started cutting a hole in the drywall. It was harder than he'd thought it would be, and the flames started to come closer to him as he worked the knife through it.

He couldn't regret that he might not make it out of the room. If he made it out, it would prove everyone wrong, prove how lucky he really was.

Finally, he had a rough square cut in the drywall. He worked quickly on doing the same on the second sheet that formed the wall in the other room. He pushed it out, just as the smoke in the room was getting to be almost too much for him.

He got lower, putting his head down near the floor and inhaling the little bit of fresh air left.

He had to wriggle around to get through the hole he'd

cut in the wall, and as soon as he was on the other side, he took out his lighter and walked to the door. He bent down and caught the carpet on fire as well before sprinting for the stairs. He kept moving quickly through the lobby and out of the building. Damn, he thought as he approached his favorite casino and heard the distant wail of fire-truck sirens.

He may have finally found something he was good at.

Jane Monte saw her life flash before her eyes as smoke filled the hallway of the forty-second floor at the Royal Banner Hotel & Casino. She didn't want her life to end like this. Alone, wearing a revealing negligee that she'd spent too much money on, and in the hotel hallway of a casino in Las Vegas.

Her parents would be sad, of course. Everyone at her funeral would say what a nice girl she'd been. What a good girl. What a tragic ending to a life that had been so perfect on the outside, but on the inside she'd known the truth. Her life could be summed up by a few paltry words. Words like *dull* and *boring*—a life filled with routines and rules.

She'd decided to throw out those rules on January 1 and had started to make changes, but now in late February it seemed like too little, too late. But she knew she'd only gone after the superficial changes, even though almost two months had passed. Clothes like this negligee replaced her ultra-conservative Ralph Lauren ensembles. Now, as she started coughing from the thick smoke, it seemed like she'd wasted every one of her twenty-nine years.

Suddenly a hand grabbed her arm and dragged her down to the floor. A water-soaked handkerchief was pressed to her nose and mouth. Disoriented, she struggled until she heard a voice in her ear.

"I'm Liam O'Roarke and I'm not going to hurt you. Just help you."

She stopped struggling, looking up into eyes that were

black as night and very calm. *Very serious.* It was hard to panic when faced with the utter confidence radiating from him. She didn't know why, but he made her feel safer.

"Crawl," he said, pushing her forward.

She started moving, trying to keep the handkerchief over her face, but she finally gave up on the handkerchief and just crawled quickly in the direction the man had indicated. She reached the steel fire door at the end of the hall and the man pressed the handkerchief to her face again.

"How did you get this?"

"I picked it up when you dropped it. When I open the door, crawl quickly over the threshold and get out of the hall-way."

She nodded.

The door opened and fresh air rushed into the hallway as smoke filled the stairwell. She moved quickly, stepping onto the cold cement. There were a few other people in the stair-well, all looking as shell-shocked as she was certain she did. Fire alarms at hotels were supposed to be the result of juve-nile pranks, not real fires.

The man who'd dragged her down the hall closed the door and then took charge of their group.

"Everyone okay? Anyone having trouble breathing?"

There was a negative murmur, and he looked at her. "I'm fine," Jane answered.

"Good. Let's get going. Straight down the stairs. Don't run. Just keep moving," Liam said.

Everyone walked and Jane followed the crowd—even though Liam had closed the door, smoke continued to fill the stairwell. At each landing she noticed that Liam checked the doors, which were locked from their side. When they reached the landing for the thirty-fifth floor, they found the door propped open. Liam motioned for them all to continue down the stairs. He took a damp hand towel and tied it around the bottom of his face, concealing his mouth and nose.

"Where are you going?" she asked, thinking it was insane not to get out of the building.

"To make sure there's no one left on this floor," he said, disappearing quickly. She couldn't argue that he was good at rescuing people—after all, he'd saved her.

What if something happened to him and he couldn't make it back to the stairwell? She didn't want to be trapped in a burning building, yet at the same time she couldn't leave him to fend for himself.

She hesitated for a second, then decided to stay behind to make sure he came back. She didn't want the man who'd rescued her to be trapped. She took the handkerchief he'd given her and tied it around the bottom of her face, just in case she had to go after him.

She glanced at her watch, which she never took off, and noted the time. Though it felt like hours had passed, it was only five minutes later when he reappeared. Just when she was about to go and see if he'd passed out in the hallway, there he was.

"What are you still doing here? I told you to go downstairs with everyone else." He untied the towel from his face and held it loosely in his left hand.

"I'm waiting for you," she said, taking off the handkerchief she'd tied on her lower face.

"Why are you waiting?" he asked.

"Because you're not Superman and smoke inhalation can affect you the same as everyone else."

He just stared at her with his jet-black eyes and then shook his head. "Come on. I'll feel better when we're all out of the building."

She followed him down the stairs and outside. She was breathing hard from the exertion and he wasn't winded at all. Looks like the resolution she'd made back in January to go to the gym should have been her top priority instead of falling off the list.

"You okay?" he asked as she paused on the small patch of grass near the exit to catch her breath.

"Just out of shape."

His eyes slid over her body and he quirked one eyebrow at her. "Doesn't look like it."

His quick grin was boyish and she couldn't help but smile back at him and shake her head.

He moved off in the direction of the fire trucks that had arrived.

"Why aren't they spraying the building?"

Liam turned back to her. "They don't have equipment that will reach above the thirteenth floor. Firefighters are already in the building using the hoses to fight the flames on the floor."

"Why didn't the sprinklers go off?"

"I don't know. I'm sure they'll be looking into that."

Liam continued toward the group of men gathered around the fire truck. Jane's breath caught in her chest as she watched the flames moving quickly across the building—nearly engulfing all of the top floors. She'd almost died.

"Hey, girl. I've been searching for you."

Jane hugged her friend, Shanna Monroe. Shanna worked for the same studio that she did, though in costuming, not publicity. Jane was in Las Vegas for an industry convention called ShoWest, where studios promoted films that would be released over the next few months. Shanna wasn't working but had driven to Vegas with her to hang out for a few days before the convention started.

"Are you okay?" Jane asked.

"Fine. I was in the casino. I knew it had to be serious when they stopped taking bets and told everyone to get out."

Jane tried to laugh but found that she was shaking too hard for that. "I was sleeping."

"It's early."

No matter how hard she tried to change herself into a

party girl, she couldn't stay up past midnight. She didn't point out to Shanna that it was two A.M., a late night by Jane's standards. "I know."

Shanna shook her head. "I'm glad we both made it out okay."

Me, too, Jane thought, but couldn't say the words. She felt that insidious panic swamping her again. Some other people they worked with were slowly making their way toward them. For the next hour they all just stood in a circle outside the hotel until the fire was brought under control and the concierge circulated amongst the guests, making alternate room plans for anyone in the affected tower.

"That's some outfit, Jane," Mitchell said. He worked in her office as one of her assistants.

She flushed and fought the urge to cross her arms over her chest. "Loan me your jacket."

He gave her a grin as he shrugged out of his jacket and handed it to her. Everyone else in her group was in a wing unaffected by the fire, but no one was able to return to their rooms. Those who'd been in the casino gambling decided to try their luck at the Bellagio just down the street. Jane declined since she wasn't bold enough to go out in her nightgown and borrowed jacket. A part of her thought this would be a great chance to finally force herself out of the old Jane mold but she couldn't do it.

As the crowd thinned and the flames were extinguished, Jane edged further from the building, hoping that the fresh air would help to calm her—but it didn't.

"You okay?"

Her rescuer again. She shook her head, unable to talk between the breaths that were sawing in and out of her lungs. She'd always had panic attacks. Her therapist thought they were due to the fact that she hated anything she couldn't control.

Even her transformation from dull Jane to exciting,

breaking-the-rules Jane was being done according to a plan she'd mapped out. In light of tonight, she wondered if her plan hadn't been another lame attempt to change her life. She'd started small—changing her wardrobe and her hair, not going after the big things that would really require her to take risks.

He pushed her head toward her knees as stars danced in front of her eyes. He rubbed the back of her neck and spoke to her in a soothing tone, though she couldn't discern what he was actually saying.

She caught her breath and stopped hyperventilating looking down at the ground and her own bare feet. She tried to lift her head but Liam kept his hand at the back of her neck.

"Give it another minute."

She stayed where she was, glancing over at his feet, which weren't bare. He wore a pair of sturdy-looking boots. When he lifted his hand a minute later she straightened and got her first good look at the man who'd rescued her twice.

He had on a pair of jeans and a button-down shirt, tails untucked. He was way taller than she was, at least six-four, and his blond hair was cut short above the ears. "Thanks."

"You're welcome. First fire?"

"Yes. Yours?"

"Ah, no. What's your name?"

"Jane. Jane Monte."

His eyes lit up and she knew where he was going a second before he got there. "No jokes. Please."

"Sorry. I have an inappropriate sense of humor."

"You do?"

He shrugged those big shoulders of his. "So I've been told."

"Well, your other actions make up for it, I'm sure."

"What other actions?"

"Saving people . . . saving me. I couldn't remember what to do when I got into the hallway." She was rambling and hadn't meant to do that at all. "So what are you doing in Vegas?"

"Vacationing. You?"

"Mixing pleasure with business."

"Sounds interesting."

"What does?"

"Your pleasure."

She flushed. She rarely flirted with anyone and certainly not a man like Liam O'Roarke.

"Sorry, that was over the line. But I couldn't resist. Let me buy you a drink to make up for it."

Normally she'd say no, because she didn't know him that well, but she'd almost died . . . okay, that was a little melodramatic, but after the night she'd had, she figured she was excused. Here was a stranger, a man she barely knew, and she was going to go for it.

"Okay. Where and when?"

"Tonight, six o'clock in the main lobby."

"I'll see you there."

Liam O'Roarke liked fire. Liked the fact that he always knew how to figure it out and get it under control. He'd spent his entire life around firehouses and had never questioned what he'd be when he grew up. There was nothing but firefighting in his blood.

He'd had one quick marriage in his early twenties, but the rest of his life was made up of fighting, drinking, and firefighting. Not much of a resumé. Not much of a future, and for a long time that didn't matter. Last year his baby sister had gotten married and suddenly Liam had started thinking of things he never had before. Things like family and the future.

So he'd taken a leave of absence from the firehouse where he worked and signed on to work with his new brother-in-law at the arson investigation firm he'd started. Andi, his sister, had come up with the name Hot Heads, Inc. He always got a kick out of the company name.

He entered the back hallway just off the casino, going quickly up the stairs to the forty-first floor where he knew the fire team was.

"About time you got here," Didi Keller said when he entered the room. The floors were water-soaked and the smell of smoke lingered. He took a deep breath of the retardant the firefighters had used to stop the fire.

It helped clear the smell of Jane from his senses and focus him back on the job at hand. *Arson.* Someone else had recently taken a liking to fire . . . or maybe the interest wasn't recent. But they'd started setting fires in the casino properties owned by Chase Banner.

Didi was an arson investigator for a national firm and had been hired by the Royal Banner Hotel & Casino's insurance company when the second fire was reported. Liam was here because the insurance company hadn't been confident that arson was involved at first, and Chase had hired his company to conduct an independent investigation.

Didi was built along Amazon proportions. Six-one in bare feet, she towered over most men in her three-inch heels. She had long blond hair that fell to the middle of her back.

When he'd first met her, he'd asked her out and been shut down. She didn't date men who loved fire. He'd shrugged and walked away because there had been an element of truth in her words. He couldn't love any woman as much as he loved his job.

He glanced around the room, looking for Chase. Chase and he went way back. Though they were working together, Chase didn't want anyone else to know. There had been four fires in the last two weeks, counting the one tonight. It looked like a serial arsonist with a vendetta against the Royal Banner, and Chase wanted it stopped.

"I do have a cover to protect," he said to Didi, accepting a flashlight from her and following her down the hallway.

"I saw you with that scantily clad woman outside. Looked like you were flirting—by no one's definition does that constitute work."

"Not when the woman's as pretty as Jane is, but if I had to flirt with you . . ."

She reached back and slugged him on the arm. "This is where we think the point of origin was."

She pushed open the charred door of one of the rooms and they walked inside.

"Was anyone staying in this room?"

"No registered guests. The sprinkler system on this floor was disabled," Didi said.

"So he wanted to make sure the fire had a chance to spread?"

"Looks like it. This sprinkler system is set up to shut down when one of the sprinklers is malfunctioning."

"Is there an alarm?"

"Yes. I need to check with security to see who was monitoring it," Didi said. "But I want to talk to the firefighters who were first on the scene."

"I'll check with security, I want to review the security tapes from here as well."

"Want to meet up later and discuss?" Didi said, as she took out her digital camera to photograph the scene.

"Yeah, maybe around noon," Liam suggested.

"Ah, I need to sleep sometime, big guy. How about later in the afternoon?"

"Sure," he said. Sleep was overrated in his book. He'd never needed more than five hours a night. When he was in the middle of an investigation, he needed even less. His mind just wouldn't shut down enough for him to actually get to sleep.

"Where's Chase?"

"Dealing with all the guests who are going to have to be relocated from this wing to one of the other ones," she said.

"I'll check in with him. I think it'd be good to meet with him this afternoon, too."

"I agree. We've detained three people who first reported the fire. I'm going to interview them when I'm done here."

Liam rubbed the back of his neck, trying to relieve the feeling that he was missing something. "I'll hit the casinos and see if I can pick up anything down there after I'm done with security."

"Any leads yet?"

Liam shrugged. "Last night I talked to Jameson Bradley. That guy really hates Chase."

"Enough to try to burn him out of business?"

"I'm not sure. But I'm going to pursue it."

He left Didi talking to the firefighters. He was careful to change out of the boots he'd worn up at the fire site. They really didn't know who their arsonist was, but Liam's gut said it was someone close to the Royal Banner.

And if there was one thing the O'Roarkes did and did well, it was read a fire.

Chapter 2

Once her room situation was straightened out, Jane's first instinct was to hole up in the hotel, but once there, she couldn't sleep. So she left the quiet safety of her room and headed toward the Bellagio, where she knew Shanna was.

The sidewalk outside of the Royal Banner was crowded and people were still talking about the fire. She tried to block out the sounds of their voices because they made it harder for her to forget that a few hours ago she was on her knees in a smoke-filled hallway, afraid of dying.

She stumbled out of the crowd and through the door at the Bellagio. Walking down the marbled hallway, she was hit with a sense of unreality. This wasn't real, she thought.

But it was. She pulled out her cell phone and sent a text message to Shanna.

Jane: *Where are you?*
Shanna: *Main casino. Blackjack table. You?*
Jane: *Coming to find you.*
Shanna: *It's after your bedtime.*
Jane: *Ha.*

She bought some chips from the cashier and entered the casino floor. It was crowded and busy. She wasn't going to be able to find Shanna easily. She might as well play some as she made her way through the casino.

She didn't know how to gamble, but hey, how hard could it be? Her younger brother Marcus had made enough money from other kids on the bus to ensure that he'd never have to use any of his allowance. And that had been in the fourth grade. She wondered sometimes how they could be birthed of the same parents.

Marcus always said she'd been born with a stick up her butt, and the words hurt. Always had, but then she knew he loved her and had said it to make her change.

And finally, at midnight on December 31, she had. She'd taken a good, hard look at herself. Sitting curled up in her flannel pajamas on her parents' living room couch, ringing in the new year while watching Dick Clark's *Rockin' New Year's Eve*, something she'd done every year. Even during her abysmal marriage, she'd still gone to her parents' house every year. Marcus had called from Rome . . . yeah, Rome. He rang in the new year somewhere new every year, and she'd envied him.

But no more. This year she was making changes . . . real changes, she thought. She scanned the casino and automatically ruled out the slot machines. She wanted something with a serious financial risk attached to it. She had to lose more than her pocket change.

She approached a blackjack table, glanced around for Shanna, and didn't see her friend. She shook her head. Was she really going to spend hard-earned money on this?

"First-timer?"

She glanced over her shoulder to see a man a few inches taller than she was. He had reddish-brown hair and blue eyes. His smile was friendly and she was suddenly very glad she'd decided to leave her room.

"To this casino," she said.

"Where have you gambled before?"

"At the Royal Banner—I'm staying there."

"Were you there earlier this evening?"

"Yes, did you hear about the fire?"

"Everyone on the Strip is talking about it."

"It was . . ." She shook her head, realizing she didn't want to talk about the fire. This handsome man might be just the distraction she needed. She gestured to the gaming room and all the different options available to those who wanted to escape from reality and take a chance on turning their own money into a fortune. "I'm still trying to decide where to start here."

"Well . . . don't say that too loud or you'll draw all the con artists out of the woodwork."

"Thanks," she said, smiling at the man. "I'm Jane."

"Nice to meet you—I'm Henry," he said, holding his hand out to her.

She took it and instead of shaking her hand, he brought it to his mouth and kissed her on the knuckles. "What do you recommend?"

"Blackjack is a good place to start," he said.

That was Shanna's game, so there was a good chance she'd find her friend at one of the tables. "That's what I was thinking. You only have to get twenty-one, right?"

"Actually, you can win with a lot less than twenty-one. You're betting on being the closest to twenty-one without going over."

"Oh. Am I playing against all the people at the table?"

"No," he said, tucking her hand through his arm and leading her to a table with two empty stools. "You're only playing against the dealer."

"Sounds simple enough," she said.

He smiled at her and it was a kind expression. They both sat down at the table. She won the first two hands.

"You're lucky," Henry said.

"I guess I am," she said, thinking of the man who'd come out of the smoke to rescue her earlier.

"No guessing about it. You should up your bets."

"What if my luck doesn't hold?" she asked.

"The table limit is fifty dollars," he said gently.

"Oh. I'm not really much of a gambler," she said.

"I can tell."

She placed her ten-dollar bet and took her cards. "Are you a gambler?"

"Yes, I am. It's in the blood."

"Really? How is it in your blood?" she asked. If that was true, then maybe she had more of Marcus's gaming luck running through her veins than she'd ever guessed.

"My family owns a few casinos."

A cocktail waitress stopped by and Jane started to order a glass of white wine, but then seconded Henry's drink request—a whiskey sour. She'd never tried one before but this was the new Jane.

"Which ones?"

"Which ones, what?" Henry said, taking two cards from the dealer.

"Which casinos do your family own?" Jane glanced at her cards—she had a ten of hearts and an eight of spades. "I'll hold."

"The Royal Banner, Athena's Palace and C&H here in Vegas, but we also own properties on the Gulf coast, in Europe, and in Asia," he said as the dealer revealed her hand—nineteen. Henry flipped his cards over, showing a five of spades and a five of hearts. "Ah, luck finally smiles on me."

"And leaves me," Jane said. "I think I'm ready to try something new."

Henry laughed. "You can't get mad just because you lose one hand."

"What do you do?"

"I keep playing until my luck changes. Give it one more hand," he said.

They played two more hands, winning one each. Then their drinks arrived. She took a sip of the whiskey sour and coughed. It was stronger than she'd expected.

"You okay?"

"Yeah," she said. "It's been a long night."

"Were you in the casino when the fire started?" Henry asked.

"No, I was sleeping in my room," she said, fishing the cherry out of her glass and eating it.

"I thought the flames were contained to unoccupied floors," Henry said.

"I don't know," she said. "My floor was filled with smoke."

"Hey, Jane," Shanna said, coming up behind her.

She turned to introduce Jane to Henry, but he was already on his feet and leaving the casino.

"Who was that?"

"Just a guy," Jane said.

"He's pretty cute. So what are you doing out past your bedtime?"

"Learning blackjack," she said, carefully taking a second sip of her whiskey sour. This time she swallowed without coughing. She got to her feet. "So what's next?"

"Mitchell is getting a group together to hit the clubs."

"I'm in," she said. Inside she knew she was moving too fast and that this wasn't real. Eventually real life was going to catch up with her . . . but until it did, she was going to live like she had nothing to lose.

Chase Banner was one of the five wealthiest men in the hotel/casino business. That wasn't a list confined to the United States—that was worldwide. It was easy to see why he was so successful. He lived and breathed for his casinos.

Though he was married and had two kids, Liam knew that Chase spent more time traveling among his properties than at home. Nothing happened within the walls of his buildings that he didn't know about.

"Did you find anything?" Liam asked, sitting down on one of the spindly-legged guest chairs in Chase's office. He sprawled his big body out, hoping his weight wouldn't crush the delicate-looking chair.

"I've been busy dealing with my guests and getting them all resettled. So no, I haven't found anything. Isn't that why I hired you?"

"Don't get testy. I'm keeping a low profile, remember? The security guy on duty wasn't someone I knew, so I just buzzed through there."

"I'll get the tapes. Sorry about lashing out. I don't need this shit right now."

"I know you don't," Liam said. "I have a few questions to ask you about Jameson Bradley."

"What about him?"

"Ah, what's up between you two? He seems to hate you."

"He sold me his run-down, crappy casino about ten years ago . . . it's the property we turned into Athena's Palace."

"Nice location," Liam said. Athena's Palace was in the heart of the Vegas Strip. "Were your dealings with him fair?"

"Yeah, they were," Chase said, rubbing his neck again. "But he doesn't see it that way. He thinks that I put the squeeze on him."

Liam laughed. "He said the exact same thing to me."

"Why are we talking about him? He has no business sense and he's lucky I came along with my offer when I did. The bank was about to foreclose."

"There are generally six motives for arson and one of them is revenge. I want to cover all the bases."

"Well, I don't know that Jameson hates me enough to burn down my casinos, but he definitely wouldn't lose any sleep if I start to suffer financially, which I am with all these fires."

"Can you think of anyone else?" Liam asked, because another motive for arson was to cover up bad finances. Chase had just implicated himself with that one comment. And though Liam and he went way back, there was no way he could ignore anyone with a possible motive to start those fires.

Chase pushed to his feet and went to the wet bar, pouring himself two fingers of Glenlivet single-malt scotch. "I've been buying up failing properties for the better part of fifteen years."

He lifted the bottle toward Liam.

"Yeah, I'll take a glass. So who else comes to mind?"

"Hell, I don't know."

"Why don't you make a list of all the properties you've acquired and I'll have the guys back in our office start doing some research on where they are."

Chase took a hard swallow of his scotch. "I'll do that."

Chase called the security office and requested that copies of all the tapes from the evening be sent up. "I'll e-mail them to you when I have them. I'd say let's review them together, but I have meetings with my security staff, the fire-alarm company, and the insurance adjuster."

"I understand. Didi and I will find the pattern. I know it seems slow going but these kinds of investigations take time."

"How much time? I can't stay afloat financially forever with my hotels catching fire every couple of weeks."

"I know, man. I know," he said, taking a sip of his own scotch.

The office door burst open and Henry walked in. "I thought the fire was contained to unoccupied floors."

"Ah, no, it wasn't. How did you hear about the fires?" Chase asked.

Henry was Chase's younger brother and the two men were as different as night and day. Where Chase lived and breathed for business deals and mergers, Henry lived and breathed for his own pleasure. He was a gambler with a serious addiction problem, and Chase had bought him out of the family business years ago. But Liam didn't know all the details of that deal.

"Everyone who's in Vegas tonight knows about them. And I'm still a Banner. I do care about what happens here."

Chase rubbed the back of his neck. "Sorry, Henry. It's been a long night."

"I can imagine." Henry glanced over at Liam. "O'Roarke, what are you doing here?"

"Hanging out," Liam said. Chase didn't want anyone, even his younger brother, to know that Liam was an arson investigator, and since he'd been a firefighter and recreational gambler for years, his cover wasn't that hard to believe. "But I was just leaving. Later."

Liam left the offices and text-messaged Didi to see where she was in her investigation. He got a terse reply that simply said *interviewing*.

She was still with the witness who'd sounded the alarm. Liam entered the casino and looked around the place. It wasn't as busy as it had been earlier in the evening before the fire.

He headed for the high-stakes poker room, hoping to find Jameson Bradley, but the other man wasn't there. The night was waning but the die-hard poker players still hung in there. Liam played a few hands and fished for any information the other players might have on the fires but came up empty.

Thinking of the fire brought Jane to mind. She had one fine body underneath that silky, see-through nightgown. She was so tempting—and so obviously into being tempted.

But he wasn't going to be seeing her until much later in

the day, and he was in Vegas to do a job. Jameson wouldn't have stopped playing poker. Not this early. And Liam knew from the game they'd had earlier in the day that Jameson was riding a winning streak.

He left the Royal Banner and cruised down the Strip looking for Jameson and the chance to question him.

The music pumped through the club. Around her were a sea of bodies and she was trying to lose herself in the moment, to just let go and forget that personal space was a huge issue for her, but she couldn't. She felt her breath catch in the back of her throat and her pulse start to race. She wished it could be attributed to lust or anything else, but she knew it was the beginning of a panic attack.

She grabbed Mitchell's hand and motioned that she'd be waiting by the bar. She signaled the bartender but knew that drinking wasn't going to help.

She left the club and found a quiet bench. The feeling of unreality she'd had earlier lifted and she saw her life clearly. This was the moment when she had to change her life.

"Jane?"

She glanced up to see Liam standing next to her. He had on the same clothes as earlier and the scent of smoke clung to his skin.

"Hey, Liam."

"Clubbing?"

"Yes. But the crush of bodies was a little too much for me."

"Is it normally or are you still shaken from the fire?" he asked, sitting down next to her.

"Shaken, I think. How'd you know?"

"You have a shell-shocked look about you. The fire wasn't out of control at any point. The fire department here is a top-rate crew."

"It isn't the fire so much," she admitted.

"What is it, then?"

"Ah, I'm not sure I know you well enough to tell you."

He gave her a half-grin that revealed his crooked bottom teeth. That tiny flaw in an otherwise perfect man made her like him a little more.

"A stranger is the perfect person to tell your secrets to. There's an entire Web site dedicated to that."

"I've heard of it."

"I'm the same thing."

She shook her head. "You are definitely not the same thing as an anonymous Web site."

"But I can be. Tell me."

She took a deep breath. "What happens in Vegas stays in Vegas?"

"Promise."

She wanted to talk to someone. Someone who didn't know her and didn't know just how mired she was in being a good girl.

"I'm . . ." Oh, God, she couldn't do it. What was she going to say? I'm the most boring woman you could ever hope to meet? "I can't. Thanks."

He rolled those big shoulders like they were tense and stood up. "I'm going gambling—want to come with me?"

"What kind of gambling? I tried blackjack earlier and it's not really my game."

"Poker—seven-card stud."

"I don't know how to play."

"I'll teach you," he said. "I'm a good teacher."

"Really?"

"Yes. I taught my brothers and sister to play."

"Are they any good?"

He gave her a narrowed look. "Patrick just won a competition last month."

"So you're all gamblers?"

"Not really. But we're all good at what we do," he said. He led her down the corridor back toward the casino.

"How many are you?"

"Five all together. Three brothers, one sister. I'm smack in the middle."

"I only have one brother, younger," she said. "He's actually one of the reasons why I'm here."

"Yeah?"

She thought about what he'd said earlier. About the safety of sharing her problems—make that *fears*—with a stranger. There was something so appealing about it.

She stopped walking and drew him out of the main walkway. "He thinks I'm a stick-in-the-mud, and I've been trying to change."

"Well, Vegas is the place to do something wild," Liam said.

"I want it to be about more than doing something wild. *You know?* I don't think getting drunk and flashing my breasts is going to change my life."

"If you want to give it a try, I'm willing to be the man you flash."

She shook her head at him.

"Are you a stick-in-the-mud?" he asked.

She wanted to say no, but the truth was . . . "Yes. I have all these rules."

"What kind of rules?"

"I don't know . . . rules for living. I've always been a good girl. Always tried to do the right thing . . . but—" Was she really going to tell him that Jonas had left her for his twenty-year-old receptionist? Ah, no. Being a stick-in-the-mud was one thing, being a loser was something else.

"But what?"

"I'm tired of being a good girl," she said. "Tired of always doing the right thing, and I thought I'd taken some steps to change my life, but instead tonight when I was in that smoke-filled hallway I realized that I'd just changed the superficial things.

"And I . . . I think that it's time I started being a bad girl."

He gave her a long, narrow look. "So what's the problem?"

"I have no idea where to start," she said, looking up into those serious dark eyes of his.

"I do," he said.

Chapter 3

Jane was a lot of fun when she forgot herself. But getting her to do that was harder than Liam would have guessed. Despite what she'd said to him, he could see that she wasn't such a dull girl. Her life may have been made up of rules, as she said, but there was such fire in her.

The kind that drew him.

He leaned into her body and took her hand in his, kissing her closed fist and then stepping back. Her eyes were wide as she glanced over her shoulder at him. Even though seven-card stud was his game, Jane had been entranced by the craps table.

"Toss the dice," he said.

She let them go and closed her eyes, as if afraid to see the outcome. He leaned into her body again, pulling her against him, waiting to see where her dice landed. "You rolled a six."

Craps wasn't as complicated a game as it seemed. And it was the one she'd chosen, blushing sweetly and telling him that she'd been embarrassed to say the name of the game.

"I won," she said, turning around and giving him a hug. "I won—I can't believe it."

The other players at the table gave her high-fives, and those who'd had their bets on the pass line at six also collected their winnings.

"Of course you won," he said. "Are you going to play again? If you roll a six again without rolling a seven, you'll be a big winner."

"I don't know. I'm tempted to take my winnings and go," she said.

"It's your decision."

"What would you do?" she asked.

The stakes she was playing for were too small to really interest him. She'd won twenty bucks but he could see the flush on her skin and the excitement in her eyes. Something that would not be helpful if she were a professional gambler—the kind he was pretending to be.

"Are you having fun?" he asked.

"Yes. I really am."

"Place your bets."

"In or out?" he asked her.

"Will you stay and be my good-luck charm?" she asked.

"I've never been lucky for anyone." He didn't really believe in the vagaries of luck. He won when he played poker because probability was something he was good at predicting. And a card game had a certain logic to it, the same way a fire did.

"You have for me, all night tonight."

He thought about what she said. Wanted to tell her that luck had nothing to do with him, but she stared up at him with such expectation. Despite the fact that she was essentially a stranger, he didn't want to disappoint her.

"Yes, I'll stay."

She put her chips on the number on the table and then took the dice from the dealer. She lifted her closed fist toward him and he brushed another kiss on her hand.

She leaned forward, tossing the dice on the green felt table, her hips brushing against his as she did so. He felt an immediate reaction. The same one he'd been trying to ignore all night.

He wrapped his free arm around her, keeping her close in the curve of his body. Her dice landed and bounced but he paid little attention to the numbers on them. All he could see was the thick fall of her hair around her ear and how the short length left the back of her neck exposed.

"O'Roarke, what are you doing out here?"

Liam was jarred back to reality with the sound of Jameson's voice. Damn, he didn't have time for Jane right now. He let his hand slide down her hip, turning to face the other gambler.

Jameson approached him with his usual entourage. "Teaching Jane how to play craps."

"I won again," Jane said, hugging him.

"Why don't you teach her how to play high-stakes poker?" Jameson asked. "The game just isn't the same without you."

"Place your bets," the dealer called.

Jane nibbled on her lower lip, clearly undecided, then shrugged and turned back to the table, placing her bet. He knew the chances of her rolling a six again were slim, and then the dice would shift to another player.

"Go on, Liam, you don't have to stay with me," Jane said, holding the dice loosely in her hand.

Despite the fact that he was pretending to be a man on vacation, he knew he was supposed to be working and he needed to talk to Jameson. But by the same token, he also knew that if he were really on vacation, he'd never leave a beautiful lady who tempted him the way Jane did.

"My daddy would skin me alive if I left a woman alone," he said.

"Perfectly understandable," Jameson said. "I'm going to be playing all day. I'll see you later, then?"

"Definitely," Liam said.

"You don't have to stay, Liam," Jane said.

"I want to."

"Oh," she said.

He lifted her fist where the dice were loosely held and brushed his lips over the back of her knuckles. "Come on, baby, keep this winning streak going."

She tossed the dice and got a nine. The people who were playing true odds were happy with the bet and the pass line bet moved to nine. The dice went to another player and Jane stared at the table.

"I don't know what to do," she said.

"Let it ride," he said. "The money will come back to you."

She did and they played for a while, time slipping away as they stood at the craps table. He stayed behind her the entire time. Her body brushed his each time she leaned over the table to place a bet or take the dice. He kept one of his hands on the curve of her hip.

He liked the way she felt in his arms, and from the easy way she rested against him, she liked it, too.

"Thanks," she said as they left the Bellagio and walked back toward the Royal Banner.

The pearly-pink fingers of dawn were slowly sweeping over the sky. The air was crisp and clean after having been in the casino. She looked tired but he could almost feel the energy and excitement buzzing through her body as they walked.

"You're welcome."

"I'm going to make a mess of this, but . . ."

"Mess of what?" he asked. She didn't say anything else.

She stopped walking and turned toward him. Standing on her tiptoes, she took his face in her hands and kissed him.

Jane was flying blind here, trying to figure out what she wanted. She pushed all of that analytical thinking out the door. She'd been thinking and analyzing and planning her entire life and for the first time she wanted to let go and just feel.

Liam's arms came around her and he drew her against his body. She was almost accustomed to feeling his hard muscles from the long night they'd spent together in the casino.

She knew he was essentially a stranger, but she didn't care. This was her piece of unreality. Her chance to really change her life and do something outrageous. Break her own good-girl biggie rule . . . no sex with a stranger.

He cupped the back of her head and drew her closer. She leaned forward and found herself within an inch of him.

Her lips suddenly felt dry, so she licked them. His eyes narrowed as he followed the movement with his gaze. His fingers stroked slowly, drawing her into a world where only the two of them existed. The hotel dropped away.

He lowered his head and this time moved his lips over hers. He kept his touch light, his lips simply rubbing over hers, tracing the seam between her lips with his tongue. She let her eyes drift closed. This felt so right that she allowed herself to be swept into the wave of passion flowing between the two of them.

He lifted his head and she opened her eyes, staring up into that serious black gaze. "What are you asking me?"

She shrugged. There was no way she could ask him to come up to her room. Why the hell not?

"Come up with me?"

He sighed and she felt the no before he said it. Didn't guys always want to have sex?

"Why not?" she asked.

"This isn't right for us."

"There is no us, Liam. We're two people on vacation in Vegas."

He shook his head. "Normally, I'd agree but you're different."

She didn't want to be. She wanted to be the kind of girl that a man would go up to her room with after a night in the casino.

"Fine. See you," she said, turning on her heel and walking away.

He stopped her with his hand on her arm. "Not so fast."

"I don't see any reason to stay."

"Are you really just looking for a quick lay?" he asked her.

His crude words jarred her. A quick flash of reality in a night that had taken on a hazy, dreamlike quality, and it reminded her that she was going to have to live with the consequences of whatever happened in Vegas. Sure, she could buy into "whatever happens in Vegas, stays in Vegas," but she was in PR and she knew that a slogan like that wasn't based in real life.

"I don't know," she said reluctantly.

"Exactly—you're riding some kind of wave. The excitement of winning at the craps table, the fear of living through the fire. You don't want me, you want . . ."

"What do I want, Liam?" she asked, because she had no idea what she wanted besides his arms around her. There was something so comforting about this man.

"I don't know, Jane. But I do know I want more than one night with you."

His words warmed her. She realized that he never had been saying no to her. But that didn't change the feelings so close to the back of her throat, that panic that she was barely keeping at bay. "I'm afraid to slow down."

The words came out of nowhere but she knew they were the truth. She was afraid to stop moving. Afraid that she was going to crumble into a bunch of little pieces if she did.

He wrapped one arm around her. "What are you afraid will happen if you slow down?"

She pulled away from him. What was she doing? Why was she even . . . "I don't know."

"Come on," he said, leading her into the Royal Banner.

The lobby wasn't too busy at this time of day. He led her across the marbled floor toward the bank of elevators. "Which floor are you on?"

"Fortieth, in the west wing," she said. She wasn't too sure about being up that high. What if there was another fire?

"Where are you?" she asked.

"I'm staying in one of the cottages."

"What are the cottages?"

"They are little guest suites nestled around the pool."

"Sounds nice," she said.

"I'll show you mine later."

He pushed the elevator call button. He was going to send her off to her room and she was letting him. What would Shanna do? Why did that matter? She wasn't Shanna and never would be. She needed to find her footing on her own. Find the new Jane that made her content to be herself.

The elevator doors opened and he escorted her into the car. "What are you doing?"

"Seeing you to your room," he said. He held her hand loosely in his and she realized she was clinging to him. That this was another kind of crutch. She was building herself around Liam. Her new self, but still—how was this different from what she'd done with Jonas when they'd first started dating?

"Oh," she said, realizing she sounded like an idiot. She dropped her hand from his. "That's not necessary."

"It is to me."

"You're a sweet man for a professed bad boy."

"I'm not sweet," he said.

Liam knew he should have said good-bye to Jane in the lobby, but he didn't want to. And unlike Jane, who seemed to overthink every action she took, he went with what he felt. And right now, every instinct he had said to stay with her and take care of her. Except he knew he was piss-poor at taking care of anyone.

There was a reason why he had been a first-class fire-fighter and was a damn good arson investigator. He didn't have to look out for anyone but himself. He only had to focus on the fire and getting control of it.

The only person he'd ever taken care of was himself. So why the hell was he staying here? What did he think he was going to do when they got to her room?

He'd already decided not to sleep with her tonight, but he wasn't ready to walk away.

"How did you know what to do in the fire?" she asked.

He shrugged his shoulders, not sure how much information about his real life he wanted to share with her. "It wasn't my first."

"Is it something you really get used to?"

"Some people do," he said, thinking of the arsonist, who-ever it was, who obviously had a taste for setting fires.

"I don't think I could," she said. "I hardly remembered to stop-drop-and-roll, and I've heard that over and over again since I was five years old."

"Everyone is disoriented in a fire," he said as they reached her floor and the elevator doors opened. They stepped into the carpeted hallway and she led the way to the right.

"You didn't seem like you were," she pointed out.

"My dad was a firefighter . . . I grew up doing drills and putting out flames."

"Oh. What was that like? My dad was a middle manager in a bank."

"It was . . ." How did he describe the old man to a stranger? His father was a larger-than-life kind of guy who believed that the only way his kids would survive to adult-hood was to know how to take care of themselves. Liam understood that the old man had to be sure they could handle themselves since he was at the fire station more than he was at home. It was part of the reason why Liam had always remained unattached.

"Is that too personal a question?"

He scrubbed his hand over his face. The last thing he wanted to talk to her about was his family. "Nah, my dad is hard to describe."

"I wasn't asking about your dad," she said.

"He's the driving force behind my childhood, so you kind of were."

"And we're strangers," she said.

"You said it."

"This is my room," she said. She pulled her key from her pocket. "Is this as far as you go?"

There was a note in her tone that made him angry. He knew that she'd regret sleeping with him if he took her to bed right now and he was willing to bet on that.

"How far do you want me to go, Jane?" he asked her, pinning her body back against the wall. He braced his hands right over her shoulders and leaned into her body until the mounds of her breasts were pressed into his chest and her hips cushioned his.

"Is this far enough?" he asked, lowering his head so that he spoke right into her ear. He rotated his hips, rubbing his growing erection against her.

He bit softly at her neck and felt the reaction all the way to his toes when she squirmed in his arms and thrust her hips back toward him.

"No, Liam, it isn't."

"What do you want from me?" he asked.

She looked up at him with those wide eyes of hers and he couldn't think of anything except that there was too much knowledge in them. That she was seeing a side of him that he didn't let anyone see. She'd found a way past his guard and he hated that.

He lowered his head, kissing her. He thrust his tongue deep into her mouth, leaving no doubt about what he wanted from her. He was angry at himself, because despite what she said here in the hall, he knew she was just using him because she didn't want to be alone. If he'd thought for one second that she really wanted him, he would have been through her hotel room door faster than a wildfire over dry land.

But she didn't.

He gentled the kiss, rubbing his lips over hers and trying to make up for his aggression just a moment ago. He skimmed his hands down her sides, holding loosely onto her hips.

"That's it, Jane. This is as far as I go right now."

She stretched up on her tiptoes, tangling her fingers in the hair at the back of his neck. She stroked her tongue over his lips and then sucked the bottom one between her teeth.

She ran her fingertip around the edge of his collar and then down his back. Cupping his butt as she let go of his lower lip.

Good God, he was on fire. Why the hell had he said that he was stopping at the door?

She scooted away from him and he followed her, reluctant to let her go.

"That's it, Liam," she said, winking at him. She pushed the key card into the lock on her door and opened it up. "Thanks for teaching me to play craps."

She closed the door and he wanted to scream with frustration. But he had to laugh at how neatly she'd gotten the upper hand on him. He would do anything to be in her bed with her. And the next time she invited him up, he was sure as hell going to do a lot more than just escort her to the door.

He walked away thinking it was a damned good thing he had an investigation to concentrate on—otherwise, he probably would have knocked on her door and begged her to let him in.

Chapter 4

Liam checked in with Didi and then crashed in his room for about four hours. He woke up refreshed and ready to jump back into the investigation. He spent two hours going over the digital copy of the security tapes that Chase had forwarded to him. There were a couple of fuzzy images he wanted to have his digital film experts take a look at.

There was no activity on the floor where the fire started, which made an odd sort of sense because those floors were under renovation. But the cameras weren't fully installed, the way they were every five feet on the occupied floors, so there were areas for anyone to hide.

He rubbed the back of his neck and forwarded the tapes to Tucker along with his initial thoughts.

His cell phone rang. "O'Roarke."

"Did you get the security tapes?"

"I'm reviewing them now, Chase. Why?" he asked. Even though he and Chase were good friends, Liam and Didi still considered the other man a suspect. They had a forensic accountant going over all of Chase's finances to prove he wasn't gaining from the fires. Since the damage to the casino was quickly reaching the million-dollar mark, Liam knew the government would soon be sending in an ATF guy to investigate as well.

"I'm reviewing some security tapes from early this morning from the west wing."

"Uh, damn." Liam had momentarily forgotten that all of the hotels and casinos in Vegas were hard-wired with security cameras that recorded everything that happened thanks to Jane. And he was surprised that Chase had been looking at a tape of him and Jane in the hallway of her hotel room.

"Just wanted to make sure you were still focused on my fires."

"Of course I am. She's got nothing to do with the investigation."

"Just a little fun?" Chase asked.

"No," he said, pushing to his feet. "Leave it the hell alone, Chase."

"Fine, I'll back off but don't forget why you're here."

"I won't forget it. You got a problem with the investigation?"

"Fuck. No. Not really. I just want answers. I want the fires to stop."

There was a level of frustration in Chase's voice that Liam hadn't heard before. He'd been convinced from the beginning that his friend had nothing to do with the fires but now he was wondering if that were true.

"I'm doing my level best, Chase. You've seen the security tapes. You know there's damned little to go on."

"Yeah, why is that?"

"I'd guess that your arsonist knows the security camera setup."

"We never get anything more than the trace of a shadow when he's moving through the hallway."

"Can you enlarge it?"

"I'm going to send it back to our office for them to analyze. That's not really my area of expertise."

"No, it wouldn't be."

"Yeah, I'm better in a fire."

"I heard that."

"From?"

"All the guests you helped get downstairs. Some of them even inquired if you were a firefighter—maybe you should watch that next time."

"I can't stand by when there's a fire."

"I know. Christ, I don't even know what to do any more."

There was a knock on his door. "Hold on a sec."

He put his hand over the speaker and opened the door and Didi walked into the room. "Ready to talk turkey?"

"I'd say we need to talk fires," he said.

"Ha. Who are you on the phone with?"

"Chase," he said, lifting his thumb from the speaker. "You want to come over here? Didi and I are going to be discussing the case and the leads we have."

"Yeah. I'll be there."

Chase hung up and he turned back to Didi. "So how'd the interviews go?"

"They were fine. No one saw anything, really."

"Who reported the fire?"

"There were two 911 calls, one from outside the hotel from Darren Addison. He's staying at Bally's and saw the flames from his room."

"Did you talk to him?"

"He wasn't in his room when I called the hotel. I did leave a couple of messages for him."

"Who was the other 911 call?"

"A maid from this hotel, Maria Gonzalez. I did speak to her and she said she smelled smoke. She was pretty straight-forward with what she knew, and her reaction was consistent with someone who'd been in a fire."

Liam pushed to his feet, pacing around the living room of his small cottage. "I didn't get a chance to talk to Jameson."

He couldn't regret that he'd chosen to stay with Jane, but a part of him was torn that he had. He wanted this arsonist caught.

"No problem. I can talk to him officially if you want. I talked to Tucker earlier and he said that he had a list of those who'd benefit financially if the Royal Banner closed."

"I haven't had a chance to look at the list yet. Is Jameson on there?"

He went over to his computer and opened the e-mail from Tucker. The list wasn't as short as Liam would have liked. There were fifteen people, and he had more than a passing acquaintance with three of them.

But then, he'd spent more than half his life coming to Vegas. "Why is Henry on here? I thought Chase bought him out."

"He still has a seat on the board of directors for the Banner Casino Group, as does Wendy Banner."

"Chase's wife isn't interested in the casinos and never has been."

"I think we're working on the theory that if there was no casino, her husband would pay more attention to her."

That made an odd kind of sense but he knew Wendy was happy with her luxurious lifestyle and didn't mind her absent husband. "I'll talk to her."

"You can't. The only person on that list that knows why you're here is Chase. I'll do the interviews this afternoon," Didi said.

Liam stood up and brushed her hands aside, massaging her shoulders. "Thanks, big guy."

"No problem. We'll get this one. I can feel it in my gut."

"Yeah? Is your gut always right?"

"Ha, poke fun all you want but when it comes to fire, I'm never wrong."

"When *are* you wrong? Rumor has it you glide through life."

As if. He'd been wrong when he'd married Dawn when they'd both been eighteen and he'd been wrong when he'd moved in with Lana at twenty-six. His instincts were honed in fire and piss-poor when it came to women.

Lush foliage surrounded the pool and there were guest cottages nestled around the area. Jane glanced at the gated pathways that led to them and told herself firmly that she wasn't hoping for a glimpse of Liam. She and Shanna were sunbathing.

"You were working the Bellagio last night," Shanna said, reaching between the lounge chairs to the small table and her strawberry daiquiri. The pool at the Royal Banner was built to resemble a tropical oasis, wisely not incorporating the medieval scheme of the rest of the resort.

Jane didn't want to talk about last night or early this morning. She longed for a work assignment. But she was on vacation, so there was nothing to think about other than the fact that she'd wanted to have sex with Liam this morning and he'd turned her down.

"Jane?"

"What?"

"I want to hear about the guy from last night."

Guy? She could only remember Liam. Tall with midnight eyes and the kind of presence that made her believe he could handle himself in every situation. "Which one?"

"The cute guy you were playing poker with."

She chose the safety of Henry, who was cute but didn't really attract her the way Liam had. "Oh, Henry. He was sweet and he knew a lot about poker." Henry was really nice but he reminded her a little too much of her ex for her to be really comfortable around him.

"Who were you thinking of?"

She sighed. She'd never in her life talked to her girl-friends about a guy she was really interested in. But Shanna had more experience than Jane did with men and a part of her was so tired of just thinking about last night. She did want to talk about it.

"Liam."

"Did I meet him?" Shanna asked. She smiled at a couple of college-age men who walked by them, each holding a bottle of beer.

"I . . . left the dance club with him. He's tall."

"That's not much of a description."

She thought about his thick blond hair, the strong cut of his jaw, and his nose, which looked like it had been broken at least once. How was she going to describe him to Shanna?

"He has blond hair."

"I didn't see him." Shanna pulled her sunglasses down low on her nose. "What's up with him?"

"I don't know," Jane said. She took her sunglasses off and looked over at her friend. If she was going to do this, then she needed to stop being so tentative. She wanted Shanna's advice. Really wanted to know where she'd misread the signals.

"He's a lot of fun and sexy as hell."

"So what's the problem?"

"I don't know. I invited him up to my room," Jane said.

"All right, Janie. How'd that go?"

"He turned me down," she said, picking up her own frothy drink and taking a sip. "I thought men never said no to sex."

"Most guys don't when it's casual. Maybe he wants more."

She shrugged her shoulders. "I don't even know what *I* want."

"Then what's the problem?"

"Me. I'm trapped between being new Jane and old Jane."

Shanna reached across the chairs and took Jane's hand. "There are not two Janes. There is only one."

Sadly, Shanna was right and she was searching for answers about who she should be. Answers that she'd always taken for granted weren't working here. "I like him. I'm trying to be bold and go after what I want, and failing miserably."

"Jane, you couldn't fail if you tried."

Yeah, right. Granted, at work she was a dynamo and got results that the studio execs really appreciated. But at work there was a game to be played with both her bosses and the media and she knew how to work that. In her personal life . . .

"So, what about you? Meet anyone promising?"

"Janie, you're not looking for someone promising in Vegas, are you?"

"No," she said firmly, trying to believe it.

"Vegas is called Sin City for a reason. No one comes here for anything permanent."

"People get married here all the time." Jane felt compelled to point that out.

"Yeah, well, they get divorced as soon as they get back to real life."

"I know."

When Shanna didn't say anything, Jane glanced over to find her friend watching her. "I really know that. It's just that old Jane isn't used to pretending that life doesn't have consequences."

"Then new Jane shouldn't, either," Shanna said. "You can't change who you essentially are."

"I want to enjoy my life. You know, Shanna, I'm so sick of being the good girl."

"That's well and good. But remember what you just said—you can't pretend there isn't going to be some fallout from your actions."

She took another sip of her drink. "Liam said something similar."

"Sounds like he saw the real you."

God, she really hoped not. "I don't like the real me, Shanna."

"Honey, we all feel that way about ourselves."

"Everyone likes you," Jane said.

"But no one wants me around for a long time. Most of my friendships only last during production and then it's on to a new project and new people."

It was odd to think that Shanna might not be happy. She had the very thing that Jane was striving for—she was a woman who lived life on her own terms. "We've been friends for almost two years."

Shanna smiled over at her and then got up when one of the frat boys who'd been by earlier waved her over. "You coming, Jane?"

She thought about it. She wasn't going to be happy being Shanna, so she knew that she had to find her own footing. "No."

Chase had nothing new to add to the investigation and wasn't really too happy to learn that he was a suspect. Liam didn't like the fact that Chase knew he was a suspect, either, mainly because then he'd stop acting normal and that would tip off whoever the arsonist was.

"For what it's worth, I'm pretty sure you're not our fire-starter," Liam said.

"Why? Because we're friends?"

"No, because I've seen you try to grill outdoors and you can't ever get a fire to stay lit."

Chase laughed. "True. Do you need anything else from me?"

"Nah, I'm good. Didi?"

"I'm good, too. I'll stop by your office later to ask you some more questions."

Chase left and Didi sat back down on the couch. "Did you mean what you said about not suspecting him?"

He shrugged. "We need him to act normal, and being a suspect will make him rethink every move he makes. If he's not the arsonist, then the fire-starter will be suspicious."

"You're right. There are so many leads in this case, I'm not sure we're ever going to get it unraveled."

He knew that was just fatigue talking. "Did you get any sleep?"

"Not yet."

"Then that's the first order of business for you," he said, tugging her to her feet and escorting her to the door.

"What are you going to do?"

"Find Jameson Bradley and see if his reaction to the fire is normal."

"Sounds good," she said, slinging her purse over her shoulder and walking up the path toward the gate that led to the pool and walkway back to the main hotel building. "I am beat but I feel like if I could just noodle the fire around in my head for a few more minutes something big is going to open up."

"It's not unless you sleep. Didn't you say that to me? You're not Wonder Woman."

"I'm not? Are you sure about that, O'Roarke? Several men have told me I am."

"Hey, what you do in your off-time is your business."

She laughed and he smiled at her. "I'll call you later and we can figure out where to meet up."

"Sounds good."

Didi walked away and Liam glanced over his shoulder, feeling someone watching him. He saw Jane lying on one of the lounge chairs and immediately knew what she was thinking.

He started over to her, wondering how he was going to

explain Didi to her, but she stood in a rush, knocking over the drink table and grabbing her bag as she walked away. He went after her.

"Jane."

"I can't talk right now."

She weaved her way through the throngs crowding the pathway leading back up to the resort. He pushed his way through them, reaching out to catch her shoulder.

"Let me go."

"No."

"I don't understand you," she said, her voice breathless.

"There's not much to understand. Didi's not . . ."

"Not what?"

"Not important to me. She's a friend." Why was he explaining this to her? Normally, the women he dated . . . weren't Jane. And he'd known that from the moment he'd emerged from checking the thirty-fifth floor and found her standing there waiting for him.

She shook her head. "I'm being silly. I know that. We spent a few hours in a casino together. We're strangers—you don't have to explain yourself to me."

Yeah, but he wanted to. That was a kick in his ass. "Where are you heading?"

"Inside. I think I've had too much."

"Sun?" he asked.

"Vegas."

He watched her carefully. "The casinos can get to anyone after a few days."

"I didn't mean the casinos," she said with a pointed look.

"Did you mean me?" he asked. He wasn't good at subtlety. Never had been.

She shook her head. "I think I meant me."

He glanced at his watch. He needed to find Jameson before too much time had passed since the fires. He needed to see his genuine reactions. But at the same time he didn't want to just wait until dinner tonight to see Jane. If she'd even see him again.

"What do you say to getting out of here for a few hours?"

"I'm not exactly dressed," she said, gesturing to her bikini-clad body.

"I noticed."

She gave him a smile that made him groan. "I'm not into the group thing, Liam."

"Didi really is only a friend."

"What'd you have in mind?"

"A surprise. Meet me in the lobby at four and I'll show you."

She gave him a long, measuring glance and he realized that this was it. If she said no now, she wasn't going to go out with him again.

"Okay. Four o'clock in the lobby. What should I wear?"

"A pair of tight jeans and a t-shirt."

"Where are we going?"

"Out of the flash and sizzle of Vegas," he said. "I'll see you then."

Chapter 5

Jane showered, changed, and got ready in less than an hour. Glancing at the clock, she contemplated lying on the bed and watching an in-room movie until she had to meet Liam. Why was she even going out with him?

She'd made a vow never to get caught on the losing end of a love triangle again. But Liam had said the other woman was just a friend, and she was beginning to sense that he wasn't a man who would lie to her.

And he was still the only man she wanted for her vacation fling.

She stood outside the bar off the lobby. She'd always had a thing about eating alone or going into a bar by herself. She'd never been able to do it and that seemed so stupid to her. The other people in there weren't going to stare at her . . . yet at the same time, her hands felt sweaty at the thought of just walking in there and ordering a drink.

"Hello, Jane."

"Henry, what are you doing?" she asked as the other man walked over to her.

"Taking a break from gambling. Want to join me for a drink?"

And just like that, she had a reason to go into the bar. She wasn't alone anymore. She smiled at him and nodded.

She knew this was cheating and not really breaking an old habit, but it felt like a gentle, easy step into change.

He led the way into the dimly lit area. There was an aquarium that ran the entire length of one of the walls, floor to ceiling, and Henry took a seat at a table right in front of it.

He signaled the cocktail waitress and ordered a scotch and soda, then sank back into the leather armchair.

"Sorry I cut out on you last night," he said. "Did you win any more hands?"

"That's okay. I didn't play twenty-one after you left. I did learn to play craps."

He took a healthy swallow of his drink and signaled for the waitress to bring him another one.

"Is everything okay?" she asked.

"Yeah. Yeah, I'm fine. I've just been in the casino all day and I get a little focused when I'm gambling."

"Did you win?"

"Ah, Jane, you're not supposed to ask a gambler that."

"I'm not?"

"No. Winners shower money everywhere."

He finished off his drink as the waitress approached with a fresh one. She took a delicate sip of her wine and watched him. If she had to guess, she'd say he didn't win big today.

"And losers?"

He gave her a heartbreaking smile and lifted his glass. "They hang out in the bar."

There was a little-boy-lost in his eyes, and she reached across the table, taking his hand in hers. "Didn't you say this was your family's resort?"

"Yeah, but I'm no longer a part-owner."

"Why not?"

He shrugged. "That's old news. Did you win today?"

"I haven't even been in the casino."

"That could get you into big trouble," he said, a teasing note in his voice.

"Really? Are only serious gamblers welcome?"

"Anyone who spends money is welcome," he said.

"I might be in trouble. I spent the afternoon lounging by the pool."

"You could be. Why aren't you shopping?"

"I don't need anything," she said. She wasn't a recreational shopper. She'd bought her new wardrobe on a trip to Rodeo Drive and she was set for at least six months. "Shopping is not my thing."

"What is your thing?" he asked.

"Work."

"That sounds boring. Don't you have time for anything else?"

"Not really. I work at least twelve hours a day, usually seven days a week."

"Why aren't you playing twelve hours a day then?"

His suggestion made a lot of sense and would fit perfectly with who she was trying to become. But she was beginning to realize that some behaviors were too deeply entrenched.

Why wasn't she playing harder? she asked herself. She refused to answer because if she said it out loud, she'd sound exactly the way Marcus had always painted her. Boring, dull, stick-in-the-mud.

"I guess I have a hard time relaxing." She took another sip of her wine.

"I have the opposite problem."

"What do you do, Henry?"

"Gamble, party—you know, live my life."

Oh, that sounded so . . . irresponsible. So meaningless. How could a man spend his life doing nothing but that? Even Marcus, who traveled all over the world, did so with a Christian-based mission organization.

"You've got a very disapproving look in your eyes, Jane."

"I'm sorry. I'm trying to change, but I can't imagine not doing anything with my life."

"What's your job?"

"I'm in the publicity department for a movie studio."

"Which one?"

"Woodbridge Pictures," she said. The company had risen to fame in the golden days of Hollywood and had survived in large part due to remaining true to their original vision of producing quality entertainment.

Henry took another swallow of his drink and signaled the waitress. She didn't want to watch him get drunk, so she stood up and pulled him to his feet. "If I'm ever going to learn how to relax, I'm going to need a lesson. Will you show me around this resort?"

"You're not going to try to reciprocate with lessons in how to work, are you? Because my older brother has already tried that and it failed."

"No, Henry. I just want to forget for a little while that I'm failing at vacation."

"Then I'm your man," he said, slipping his hand into hers and leading her out of the bar.

Liam heard the sound of Jane's voice before he saw her. He was at a high-stakes poker table, fishing for information from Jameson, but the other man was deep in a winning streak and wasn't chatting. Liam glanced at his own hand and realized he needed to start concentrating.

They were playing No-Limit Hold 'em. Liam had first played this game when he was five years old around a table in the firehouse where his dad worked. They'd played for pennies back then but he'd learned valuable lessons at that table, lessons he never forgot when he was in Vegas.

Sometimes it made more sense to throw away a winning hand and keep playing than to go all in and lose. Jameson was riding a streak, and though it would seem to the casual observer that he was on a winner's high, Liam watched the shrewd way Jameson concentrated on the game.

He knew the odds and the cards that had been dealt and wasn't taking a chance on losing by staying in without a sure winning hand. Like all gamblers, Jameson had tells but Liam hadn't played with the other man long enough to learn them all.

"In or out, O'Roarke?"

He glanced over the red velvet ropes that kept the area separated from the rest of the casino and saw Jane with Henry Banner.

What the hell was she doing with Banner?

She smiled over at him and he tried to smile back but a flash of unexpected jealousy made that impossible. He put his cards on the table. "I'm out."

His hand had been for shit anyway because his mind was on the fire and that list of suspects instead of on poker. And unexpectedly, on Jane.

"Will you be back?" Jameson asked.

"Yes, I'm going to see if I can find lady luck and coax her back to my side of the table."

Jameson laughed. "I've never had much success with that."

"It's not hurting you."

"True, but then nothing can stop me these days. I'm on fire."

"That you are," Liam said, walking away. Jane wasn't smiling when he approached her and Henry, and a part of him acknowledged that he had no right to be angry with her for enjoying another man's company.

But his gut didn't give a rat's ass about that.

"Liam, how's it going, man?" Henry said, offering, Liam his hand.

He shrugged at the poker table. "I've had better days."

"This is Jane . . . I'm afraid I don't know her last name. Jane, this is Liam O'Roarke. He's a frequent visitor here and a friend of my family."

"We've met," Liam said, holding his hand out to Jane. She shook it once, then dropped his hand.

"Hey, Henry, we've got an open seat," Jameson called over to them.

Henry glanced at Jane. "Um . . . do you mind?"

"Not at all. Thanks for showing me around the resort."

"You're welcome. Later, Liam."

Henry joined the game.

"I know it's a little early," Liam said, "but are you ready for our date."

"Yes," she said. "That thing with Henry . . ."

He wanted to say it was none of his business but that simply didn't sit right with him. "Yeah?"

"He's a nice guy but he drinks a little too much."

Henry had a serious addiction problem and it wasn't to alcohol, so Chase and the rest of his family usually gave him a pass when he drank too much. But a woman like Jane . . . he was just getting to know her, but he felt she was the kind of woman who'd kill herself trying to save a man like Henry.

"Are you serious about him?"

She shook her head. "I'm in Sin City, Liam . . . I'm not serious about anyone."

Those words sounded false falling from her lips and he didn't buy them. But he wasn't one to argue with the lies people told themselves. He had his own that kept him sane.

"Henry's a nice guy but his life is a mess," Liam said. "Just remember that."

"What about you, Liam O'Roarke? How's your life?" she asked.

A mess. But not the kind that Henry's was. "I'm doing okay. Better, now that I'm with you."

She flushed as he put his hand on her back and directed her out of the casino. Her jeans weren't skintight as he'd imagined they would be, but the cut flattered her. They were low-riding and he felt the smooth expanse of her skin under his hand.

As they stepped outside, she reached into her purse to pull out a pair of sunglasses and her shirt rode up.

He traced his finger over the skin of her lower back, and felt her shiver under his touch.

Jane might think she needed lessons in how to relax but he had a sneaking suspicion that she already knew how and was only afraid to act on those impulses.

"I like this."

"I do, too."

"I'm on to you."

"Really?"

"There's more to you than meets the eye."

"That's true of everyone," she said carefully.

He led her across the parking lot to a Harley Electra-Glide classic. The bike had a seatback for the passenger, something he thought would make Jane a little more comfortable.

"Uh, what's this?"

"My surprise."

"I've never been on a motorcycle before, and to be honest, I don't think I want to."

"It's up to you. But you did say you wanted to try new things," he said.

She glanced at the bike and then up at him. "Are you a safe driver?"

"I promise you'll be safe with me," he said.

He saw the answer in her eyes a moment before she nodded her head.

* * *

Jane leaned back in the seat as the wind rushed around her and they headed toward their destination. Liam didn't volunteer the location and she hadn't asked. This was more surreal than the casinos in Vegas.

Her brother would never believe she was riding on a motorcycle. He'd tried to get her to ride on his more than once. Normally she thought they were too dangerous, but with the wind swirling around her and the sun shining down on them, she wasn't worried.

"My brother will never believe this," she said. Liam had rented them helmets with headsets so they could talk while they were riding.

"Believe what?"

"That I'm on a motorcycle. I can't believe it, either. It's so not like me."

Jane realized she was still talking out loud and shook her head. "I'm in a weird headspace right now—please ignore my last comment."

"Sure. How much longer do you have on your vacation?" They left the city and started driving along a smooth stretch of highway. She'd driven to Vegas, so she knew how the city seemed to sprout out of nothing. A booming metropolis surrounded by empty land.

"Three days. But I'm staying in Vegas for ten more days." She couldn't wait to get back to work. The convention would be one of the easier jobs she did. Talking about the upcoming movies on the studios production schedule was something she truly enjoyed.

"Are you going to be working a convention?"

"Yes. ShoWest."

"I'm not really familiar with that one. It has something to do with the film industry, right?" he asked.

She thought about getting back to work in a few days and couldn't wait. When she was working, the fact that she hadn't changed didn't bother her. On the job, she was competent and hardly ever screwed up. Not like real life. "It is a motion-picture industry convention. I'm in PR for Woodbridge Pictures."

"I haven't heard of them."

"Um . . . they're one of the larger studios," she said, naming a few of their box-office-topping films.

"I'm not really into movies," he said.

That didn't surprise her. He seemed so much more a man of action than a man who'd watch other people doing stuff. She loved movies because for a few hours she got to experience what it was like to live a different life, but Liam struck her as a man very secure with the place he had in the world.

"What *are* you into, Liam?"

He shrugged. "My job."

"What do you do?"

"This and that. Have you ever been to Hoover Dam before?"

"No. But we studied it when I was in school. I know it was built during the Depression. But I'm really more interested in you."

"There's not much to tell. My dad and siblings and I are pretty close. We all live within a couple of hours of each other. My little sister lives the furthest away from us."

There was a note in his voice when he spoke about his sister that she couldn't identify. "Are you an overprotective older brother?"

He seemed the type that would be.

He gave a short laugh. "Yeah, even though Andi can take care of herself, I still worry about her."

"I'm that way with my brother."

"Does your brother cause you a lot of worry?"

"Yes. He's always traveling to places that seem dangerous. I just want him to be home and safe."

"Safety's important to you?"

"Isn't it to everyone?"

He shrugged. "I think if you know how to look out for yourself—you're good."

"But even knowledge can't protect you all the time. I mean, look at the fire the other night. If I hadn't woken when I did . . . I don't think we'd be having this conversation."

"Life is random," Liam said. "There's no rhyme or reason for why people die. It just happens. You can't spend your life worrying over what might have happened, Jane."

"Maybe *you* can't," she said under her breath.

"That's right, I can't," he said.

"You weren't supposed to hear that."

"The mics in the helmets are very sensitive."

"I just figured that out."

She didn't say anything as he put more miles between them and Vegas. Life was random—that was what he'd said but she didn't buy it. She'd been planning her life since she'd turned twelve, and aside from her ex-husband Rodney's infidelity, the rest of it had gone according to plan.

But there was her ex . . . there was the moment of chance that had altered her well-ordered life. So now she was here, on the back of a Harley-Davidson motorcycle, with a man she hardly knew.

And that didn't seem to matter. She thought about how hit-and-miss life could be and scooted forward on the seat, doing what she'd wanted to from the moment she'd seen the motorcycle. She wrapped her arms around his chest and eased her body into his back.

He brought one gloved hand to cover hers but didn't say anything, and she was grateful for that. Because she didn't want to think anymore. She wanted to just experience life and the chance it had given her on this day.

Chapter 6

Liam always felt small standing on the walkway of the Hoover Dam. That was a hard thing for a man who was six-five to feel, but there was something about all that water and the immensity of the dam itself.

Jane's small hand in his made him feel big and tall and made him want to make promises that he knew no man had a chance of keeping. Promises that involved protecting her and keeping her safe.

But almost from his first conscious memory, Liam had realized that no one could be kept safe. Probably it was learning about death so early, hearing his father talk about different fires and how lives were lost. The old man had done a damn good job of making sure all his kids understood that life didn't come with guarantees.

The wind whipped around them, the breeze cooler than it had been in Vegas. It stirred the short length of Jane's hair, blowing the longer strands across her face.

She shivered, wrapping her arms around herself. He drew her against his body, hugging her close. The strands of her hair brushed across his face. They were soft and cool and carried the elusive scent of Jane.

She tipped her head back and he saw the questions in her eyes. Knew enough about women to know that she had something on her mind and she needed to talk about it.

But he wasn't thinking right now, he was feeling. Feeling her curvy body in his arms and enjoying that.

"This doesn't feel random," she said. "This feels solid and—"

He kissed her to quiet the questions that he knew would have to follow. They were vacationers and shouldn't be talking about anything other than what he heard the other tourists talking about.

The facts of the dam. How big the sky looked. And should they risk more money on the Vegas casinos? But not Jane. She wasn't like the other people who took a break from reality and just vegged out.

He lifted his head.

"What is it you don't want to talk about?" she asked.

"Nothing. I'm an open book."

She shook her head. "I know better than to believe that."

She brought her hand up to his face, traced a finger down the line of his jaw and then further down his neck. She traced over the scar at the base of his neck. It was thick and rough compared to the rest of his skin.

"How did you get this?"

It was a three-inch cut from a piece of flying debris. He'd gotten it when he'd been a first-responder at the scene of an accident. He'd been off duty but he'd felt compelled to stop when he'd seen the two cars collide. The shrapnel from the windshield had hit him as he ran toward the car to try to help the driver out.

"Car accident," he said, letting her decide what that meant.

She continued caressing that part of his neck and it was having a pronounced effect on the rest of his body. She turned in his arms, putting her hands on his hips and leaning into him, her head resting on his chest right over his heart.

"You've had a lot of brushes with death?" she asked him.

He had but he didn't want to go into that. The times

when his oxygen pack had failed or when he'd stayed in a burning building too long searching for survivors. "The scar makes that cut look worse than it was. It wasn't life-threatening."

She shook her head. "I don't have a single scar."

"That's not a bad thing."

Again he had the feeling that she was lost. That somehow she didn't know who she was and she was searching for something more. Some kind of meaning or truth in her life. That was the thing he'd never gotten. Life wasn't about analyzing and figuring out. Life was full-on moving and never stopping.

"I've spent my entire life sitting inside and looking out. You know what I mean?" she asked, then stepped back and shook her head. "No, you don't know what I mean."

She'd said earlier that she was in a weird headspace, but this made no sense. From what she'd said he knew that she wasn't sure of herself. His way of living wasn't any better than hers. It was just the way that he operated.

"Don't do this. We're different people."

"Yeah, one of us exciting . . . the other boring."

He shook his head. "What happened to make you view yourself that way?"

She shrugged, but didn't pull away. A line of Japanese tourists crowded close to them, trying to take pictures.

"Come on, Jane, tell me. It can't be any worse than when you asked me to show you how to have fun."

"Is that what I did?"

He wasn't about to let her tease him away from this conversation. "Yes. And I think I'm doing a good job of it."

"Well, craps was fun—and I won."

Winning was very important to him and he could tell it was to Jane, too. Maybe that's why she was so determined to change who she was. "Winning is always important."

"True. The jury's still out on the motorcycle."

"Liar."

"Liar? The truth is very important to me."

"Then maybe you'll recall molding yourself to my back and putting your arms around me."

"What's that got to do with anything?"

"Babe, you know you liked it," he said.

"Maybe."

"There's no maybe about it."

"You think way too highly of yourself if you think that every time I touch you it means something."

He cupped her face and leaned down to look into her eyes. "No, Jane, I think highly of you. And you don't reach out to just anyone."

"You don't know me well enough to know that."

"Yes, I do," he said.

A family of four posed in front of the dam. The father glanced around the crowd and approached them.

"Will you take our picture?" a man asked Liam. He nodded and took the camera from the tourist, who stood near the edge of the dam with his family. Liam glanced through the viewfinder and snapped the picture.

"Want us to take one of you and your girlfriend?"

"Yeah. All I have is my camera phone."

"My son knows how to operate those," the man said, gesturing to his teenaged son.

"Come on, Jane," he said. She came back over to him and he pulled her into the side of his body, looking down at her and not at the camera.

"Got it."

"Thanks."

He pocketed the phone, not looking at the photo. He'd want to later when he was alone. Not while he was still in Vegas, but once he got home and Jane went back to her real life.

Liam wrapped his arm around her waist and led her down the path toward the parking lot and the bike he'd rented for the day.

Liam pulled off the road when they were about halfway between Vegas and the Hoover Dam. He loved the vastness of the landscape in Nevada. He wasn't an outdoors nut like his older brother Patrick, who took all his leave time at once and disappeared into the Everglades for weeks. Living off the land and "getting back to nature." But on evenings like this, with the sun setting in the west and hardly any traffic on the road, he could understand some of what drew Pat to nature.

"My brother would love this place," he said.

"He's never been out here?" Jane asked, her arms wrapped around his waist. They were very close, but he wanted to feel her silky hair against his neck. Wanted so much more than they could have here on the side of the road.

But not everything with Jane had to be about sex. Too bad his body didn't agree. He wanted her. He wanted her now, and he didn't particularly like the fact that he was thinking about her more than he was about the arsonist he was supposed to be catching.

Even though he knew he wasn't letting the investigation slip, he knew deep inside that he wasn't giving his usual one-hundred-ten percent. But when he felt her arms around him, somehow that didn't seem to matter.

"No. He's never left Florida," Liam said, pulling off his helmet and hanging it on the handlebars. He turned on the seat and loosened the chin strap of Jane's helmet.

"Is that where you're from?" she asked, taking her helmet off.

He took it from her. "Yeah, I am. South Florida, near Miami."

She didn't have sunglasses on so she watched him with those wide brown eyes of hers that made him realize he was never going to figure out all her secrets.

"I'm from California. I've never been to Florida," she said.

He wanted to bring her to his home and show her the Atlantic Ocean, which was only a few feet from the ramshackle house he'd purchased more than twenty years ago. All around him, developers had purchased the property and developed it into high-rent condos, but his little place still felt like Florida to him.

"I guess you wouldn't need to, since you've got beaches and theme parks in California."

"True. I don't travel much. Do you?" she asked.

With the new job as an arson investigator, he was traveling more than ever but he didn't like it. He missed his house and the routine of his life at the firehouse. But she couldn't know about that. He shrugged, trying to find something to say that wasn't a lie. "Not really. Some for different poker tournaments."

"Is that how you make your living?"

It was getting harder to keep from talking about his job but he knew better than to trust a stranger. Especially one he'd met during a suspicious fire. Not that he thought Jane had anything to do with setting the fire at the hotel, but he didn't know if she could keep her mouth shut.

"No, it's not. I'm not really good enough to live off what I make at the tables."

He put down the kickstand and got off the bike. Standing next to her, he realized that the real reason why he'd gotten them out of Vegas today had nothing to do with her and everything to do with him. He needed to distance himself from the investigation to get his mind thinking in different ways.

Too bad he wasn't really thinking about anything other

than the way she'd felt pressed against his back. And how desperately he wanted to feel her pressed against him, completely naked.

"Why are we stopping?"

"Wanna try driving?"

"I'm not sure."

He waited, knowing that Jane didn't make snap decisions. "I'll be right behind you the entire time."

"What if I make us crash or something?" she asked, nibbling at her bottom lip.

"Life's tough sometimes. I can help you steer through anything."

"Okay. Tell me what to do."

He gave her a quick lesson on driving the Harley and then sat down on the bike behind her. He put his hands over hers on the throttle and the brake on the handlebars.

He was wrapped around her body. He really wasn't thinking of anything but the way the curve of her buttocks felt nestled into the notch of his thighs. But when she pulled the throttle back and he felt the roar of the motor of the bike in every fiber of his being, he snapped back to focus.

She was stiff and kept the bike at about forty miles per hour. Way too slow. He leaned into her and put his hands over hers, pulling the throttle back and sending them rocketing down the freeway.

Her weight shifted until she rested more fully against him, and he forgot about everything but the feel of the wind against his skin and the woman in his arms.

But as they approached Vegas, she slowed the bike and pulled onto the shoulder. "I think you should drive in the traffic."

He switched places with her without saying a word, but he was very aware that his escape from his real world had ended. Now that he was back in Vegas, Jane had to take a backseat to the investigation.

He struggled for a way to tell her, but in the end he knew he wasn't going to say anything. Because with her, he wanted to say too much. He drove them to the grand façade that was the Royal Banner. Built like a medieval castle, the hotel stood out amongst the Pyramids, Eiffel Tower, and other flashy hotels.

He got off the bike, tossing his keys to the valet. Jane stood awkwardly to the side and he started over to her, wanting to reassure her, but then he realized she was staring at someone else. Didi was standing just inside the doorway. She had two firefighters with her, which wasn't a good sign.

Didi waved him over as soon as she saw him, which was itself a sign that something had happened while he'd been out with Jane. Something significant to the investigation.

"I've got to . . ."

"Yeah, I know. Go on. Thanks for the ride."

There was real pain in her voice and he ached for her. Wanted to wrap his body around her and cushion her from the emotions she felt right now, but knew he was the one responsible for her shock.

Jane was the first to admit that she wasn't completely embracing her new bad-girl persona, but watching Liam walk away from her after all they'd shared was just the incentive she needed.

She put her sunglasses on, tousled her hair to alleviate some of the helmet-head she was sure she had, and walked right past him like she didn't care.

That's because she really didn't. She was tired of being the kind of woman who played by the rules and always ended up hurt. That was why she'd decided to change, but she was coming to realize that even not abiding by those rules wasn't exactly a guarantee that she wouldn't end up with a broken heart.

"Jane?"

Her boss, Josef Hemlich, and two other executives from Woodbridge were clustered together. Josef traveled in a pack with the other executives at the studio, always trying to stay one step ahead of what they needed. Together, those four were responsible for every project the studio green-lighted.

"Hello, Josef. What are you doing here?" She tugged her hair behind her ear and pulled on the professional persona she always wore at work. This was the one area of her life where she knew who she was. She was damned good at publicity.

"Looking for you, actually—the front desk wouldn't give me your room number."

"Sorry about that. I didn't realize you'd be arriving today." She wasn't too sorry, because she didn't want her room number given to just anyone.

"This was a spur-of-the-moment trip. First of all, are you okay? I saw the news of the fire on the TV."

"Yes. I'm fine. Everyone on our staff who came early made it through the fire okay as well."

"Good to hear that. Are you free now? We've had a situation develop. I tried calling you earlier."

Technically she was still on vacation, but that wasn't exactly working out like she'd hoped so she smiled at her boss. "I'm sorry I didn't have my phone with me," she said.

"We've got an opportunity I want you to take advantage of. We can talk about it up in my suite."

She caught Liam's gaze as she walked through the lobby with her boss and his entourage and felt the sizzle associated only with him. But she kept moving toward the bank of elevators, breaking eye contact and saying good-bye to whatever might have happened between the two of them.

She felt a twinge of disappointment in both herself and him as she moved toward the elevators.

But Liam left his "friend" and walked toward her. There was something in his eyes that warned her he wasn't coming over to meet her boss. Excitement and adrenaline vied for control of her body, much the same way as they had when she'd been driving the motorcycle.

She made the quick decision to put work off for a few more minutes.

"I've got to grab my notepad and my BlackBerry from my room. What's your suite number, Josef?"

He gave it to her as the elevator doors opened. Damn, he was staying in the same wing as she was. "I'll see you in a few minutes."

Liam arrived just as the doors closed.

"What do you want?" she asked.

"To make sure you know we're still on for tonight," he said.

"I can't. That's my boss and he needs me."

"He needs you? You're on vacation."

"Yeah, well, it looks like that's over." And none too soon, she'd been thinking. But now, she thought, maybe it was too soon.

"Tell him you have plans."

"It doesn't work that way, Liam. I should think you would be happy that I'm not going to be hanging around."

"Jane—"

"Don't. I don't want to hear any kind of story you think I'll buy."

"I'm not lying to you," he said with a direct look.

"You're not leveling with me, either. Listen, I've been lied to by men much better at it than you are."

"Fuck that. I'm not lying about anything that's important to you and me."

"I'm not sure there is a you and me," she said. She shook her head to clear it. "It's not you, it's me. I'm just not . . . that is to say, this isn't working the way I wanted it to."

"What isn't?"

She shrugged because she really wasn't going to say any

more. His actions made it easier for her to just walk away. To do it now before she started believing the half-truths he was telling her. "Whatever chimera I thought Vegas was."

She walked back to the elevator bank and pushed the call button. "Thanks for the ride. It was wild and different and for a minute I felt like I was really living."

She turned away and then realized she was still living her life by rules. Her own rules. All buttoned-up and afraid to take a risk. And Liam was a risk because she had absolutely no idea what to do with him.

She pivoted and crossed the distance between them. People were gathering to wait for the elevator and she almost let that stop her, but they were strangers. She opened her purse and took out one of her business cards. She couldn't believe she was going to do this, but she thought maybe there was something he was hiding. Knowing they were in Vegas and everything was temporary would insulate her a little from falling for him.

"Call me later about dinner," she said, and walked away.

Chapter 7

Liam scrubbed one hand over his eyes as he walked through the demolished forty-fifth floor of the Royal Banner hotel. It had been over twenty-four hours since the fire. He and Didi were going over the site one more time, walking the path of the fire and trying to put the pieces of the puzzle together.

The smell of smoke was heavy but nothing like it had been last night. Fire, which had always been as necessary to him as breathing, took a backseat to the relationship that was complicating his life.

He cursed under his breath.

"That doesn't sound like a man on vacation," Didi said.

He squatted down to photograph some of the rubble—ceiling tiles that had fallen and were charred. "I'm working."

"The investigation is not going that badly."

"It's not going great, either. I can't believe that this area wasn't secured."

"That's not something we're in charge of," she said.

"No, but Chase should have taken care of it," he said. The fact that he hadn't made Chase look like he was hiding something up here. It was the main reason they'd come back up to go over the site again.

That and the fact that once everything stopped smoldering, sometimes clues could be found that were overlooked immediately after the fire.

"Do you think he's our fire-starter?"

"Hell, I don't know. I would have laid down good money that he wasn't."

"But not now," Didi said.

He shrugged his shoulders and kept moving around the site. Didi had been waiting for him earlier because of the new footprints in the ashes up here. She had taken one look and known what he saw now, that someone had been poking around upstairs. They bagged up some evidence.

"What are we missing, Didi? Did someone take something or was it simply curiosity?"

"I wish I could tell you. I can't get into the head of our arsonist. The fires feel random."

He had to agree. There was no real pattern to the fires and each one had been started in a different way. Normally an arsonist found one type of fire and kept setting them the same way.

He cursed again, walking the perimeter of the room.

"You okay?"

"Fine."

He wasn't one of those touchy-feely guys who talked about his emotions or his problems. And since when did a vacation fling have problems? Since Jane. God, that woman had him tied in knots and he didn't think he could explain it to anyone.

He took a picture of the pile of rubble at his feet and then pushed aside a piece of debris and bent down to examine the remaining rubbish on the floor. Something metal was in the pile.

He took two more pictures as he moved stuff aside before he completely unearthed the object. He brushed it off and lifted it—a fire didn't leave behind any fingerprints. It was a charred strap like something from a backpack.

He heard Didi walk over to him, felt the weight of her hand on his shoulder as she knelt down beside him.

"Is this our ignition?" she asked.

"I think so," he said, poking around the rest of the remains as a vision of the fire played out in his mind. Only close analysis would prove him right, but he felt the first sense of what had happened here. Felt that there were rags dampened with gasoline left in this pile and then ignited with this lighter.

Liam handed the strap to Didi to put in a plastic bag to send to the lab. Once they knew the type of item they were dealing with, they could see if it matched anything found at the last two fires.

"Is this enough for a pattern?" Didi asked.

"We'll have to wait and see what the lab says." His dad had taught him patience when it came to fires. They might blaze quickly and steadily but the only way a smart firefighter could get ahead of one was by being methodical and thinking things through.

Maybe he should apply the same logic to Jane.

She got to him the same way a fire did. She tied him up in knots and confused the hell out of him but if he stopped chasing after her like she was a hot spot, he might be able to find his footing. Might be able to really figure out how to unravel her.

He pushed Jane out of his mind and focused instead on the fire. Until he got what he needed from this room and really figured out the fire, he wasn't going to be able to concentrate on her.

He heard Didi stand up and start walking carefully around the room. He noticed that she had her eyes half-closed. Did she have a bead on their fire and the burn pattern? He stood back to watch her work and realized she was following a secondary burn.

"He set three fires," Liam said, just as Didi bent down to examine another pile of wreckage.

"This is new. The other fires only had one ignition point," Didi said. She knelt down near the rubble and unearthed a second ignition point.

Liam bent down to inspect it. "He tried to use a mattress to get the blaze started."

An image flashed in his head of this room the way it had been before it had been touched by the fire. This floor was almost ready to be reopened for use. "Was this a double-double room?"

Didi opened her notebook and flipped through the pages. "Yes. So why didn't he set both beds on fire?"

"I don't know. Maybe the fire wasn't burning fast enough with the cloth?"

He walked around the room, looking for the place the arsonist would have stood while waiting to be sure the flames took and the fire would spread. He found it near the window, on the floor. The metal frame of the room was all that remained—the drywall and internal wall structure was burned out. But what remained was a clear cut in the framing.

"I've got it," he said.

Didi came over to him and they both examined the mark. They followed it through the other rooms that had been burned on this floor until they came to the fire wall. There was no cutting through this. But they could see where an ax was used to cut open the door on the last room. The splintered pieces were charred but not entirely burned.

"Well, there's one question answered," Liam said. "Now we just need to figure out how he knew how to disable the sprinkler system and how easy it was to get access to it."

The meeting with Josef lasted well into the evening and her cell phone stayed silent. She concentrated on what he wanted her to do. The movie they were putting all their promotional power behind was *Dirty Vegas*, a story of a group of con artists coming back to Vegas. It was an action-packed drama with a cast of Hollywood's up-and-coming hotties.

Josef's idea was essentially to get as much pre-ShoWest promotion as they could by staging events around Vegas with the cast and showing them imitating their characters' actions. "Most of the wheels are in motion. I just need you to coordinate with the press and set up some interviews in all the major outlets."

She took notes and smiled at her boss, knowing his idea would do a lot to promote a movie that was iffy to explain at best. They'd been struggling for weeks for a way to promote it because it was part action flick, part drama. And the media wasn't always on board with interviewing characters instead of actors, though it had worked wonderfully well for Sacha Baron Cohen and his character Borat.

"I'll get to work on this right away."

"Good. I want to see our guys on *Today* or *Good Morning America*. Then book them on Leno and Letterman."

"They are already booked on Letterman for the week prior to release."

"Great. You run with this idea and then send me the schedule."

"Where is the cast?"

"On their way to Vegas as we speak. They are using the Mustang from the film to drive here."

"Perfect. Is there a film crew with them?"

"No."

"Well, we need to shoot some film we can use of the trip—either that or use one of the actual scenes from the movie. We'll send that out to the entertainment programs. Have they left L.A.?"

"About twenty minutes ago."

"Can you ask them to stop? I think we can get one of the reporters to ride along with them."

Josef had his phone out of his pocket and up to his mouth before she finished talking. She moved away from him and took out her own phone, calling a friend of hers, Eva Mills, at *Backstage Hollywood*. The nightly syndicated show was the lowest-rated one, always struggling to keep up with *Entertainment Tonight* and *Access Hollywood*.

"Hello, Jane."

"Hey, Eva. How'd you like an exclusive scoop?"

"Uh, with who?"

"The cast of *Dirty Vegas*. Four super-hot, young, up-and-comers on a road trip to Vegas to pull off the biggest grift of their young lives."

"Maybe. When?"

"Maybe? We're talking Alan Powell, James Manners, T.J. Scallan, and Devon O'Neil. Eva, this is the interview of a lifetime. We are going to give you the exclusive rights to this ride, along with the characters of the movie. You'll be able to see these guys in character. And we're only making this offer to you."

"When are they leaving?"

"This afternoon."

"Let me check a few things and I'll call you back."

"Okay, Eva, but I've only got ten minutes."

"All four guys?"

"Yes, in character," she said.

"What would I ask them? I don't know their characters."

She was losing Eva. "I can fax you backgrounds and bios. This is an exclusive, the kind of story that *Extra* would jump at. If you aren't interested I can give them a call."

Jane heard papers shuffling. "Okay. Where do I meet them?"

She hit the Mute button on her phone, turning to Josef. "Where should she meet them?"

"Who is it?"

"Eva Mills, *Backstage Hollywood.*"

"Can't we do better than them?"

"Not with this kind of notice. Plus, I gave her an exclusive, so they'll run with it. I'll line up the other shows for here in Vegas."

"They'll pick her up at her office."

"Got it," Jane said. She unmuted the phone. "They'll be at your office in an hour."

She finalized the arrangements with Eva and hung up the phone. She was glad Mitch was in town because she was going to need him to work his connection at MTV and see if they could get some airtime.

"Okay, the ball is rolling, Josef. Give me a few more hours and I'll have a plan to you."

"Good. I've got dinner with some of our Japanese investors. E-mail me the plan. Make sure you copy the rest of my executive staff."

She picked up her purse and headed out the door, then walked down the hallway to the elevator. She had work to do, she thought. Plenty of time to do it. She'd have to call her staff in L.A., but from what Josef had said, they were ready for her.

She spent the next two hours on the phone talking to everyone in the news industry, setting up interviews, calling in favors, and doing her job. But the one person she didn't talk to was Liam. And she tried not to let that bother her but deep inside she knew that it did.

Liam knocked on Jane's door, not sure what kind of reaction to expect. He wanted to come clean with her about the investigation, but the fewer people who knew the truth of what he was and why he was here, the better it was.

But there was an ache in the middle of his chest whenever he thought about that look in her eyes. He'd made it a policy not to lie outright to anyone, but he had spent the majority of his life telling little half-truths. It was just easier when dealing with the real thing. And he did consider himself a truthful man.

The door opened and Jane stood there with her Bluetooth in one ear and in her bare feet.

"Why are you here? I thought you were going to call," she said. She didn't step back and invite him in, so he took a step forward and forced her to move.

"You thought wrong," he said, closing the door behind him and walking in. It was a standard room with two queen-sized beds. One of them was littered with papers and her laptop was open. The other one was still neatly made.

"You were serious about working?" he asked.

"Yes. I'm glad, actually. Now I don't have to feel inadequate because I'm staying up in my room."

He stroked his finger down the side of her face, pushing the Bluetooth earpiece off of her ear and tossing it on the bed. "You aren't inadequate."

She shrugged. "Not when it comes to my job."

"I'm not doing a good job of showing you how to relax, am I?"

She turned away from him and walked to the windows that overlooked the Vegas Strip. "This is better than relaxing."

He knew it wasn't. He walked over behind her and put his arms around her waist, drawing her back against his body. He lowered his head so he could rest his chin on her shoulder.

"What do you see out there?" he asked softly.

"I don't know anymore. It's not the same as it was the first night I was here. Why do you keep coming back?"

He tucked a strand of her hair behind her ear, and then brushed a kiss against her neck. "I like the fact that the city never sleeps. That no matter what I want to do, its available 24/7."

"That just doesn't do it for me," she said, her hands resting over his.

"I'm sorry, but I don't think I'm ever going to be like that."

"I'm not expecting you to be."

She pulled out of his arms and stepped away from him. "I'm making this too complicated."

"How?"

"I wanted you to be a stranger who I could have anonymous sex with and then forget. A kind of right of passage from the good girl I've always been to the bad girl I want to be. But you're not a stranger to me anymore. And I'm not so sure I want—"

"This isn't about being a stranger," he said.

"It's not?"

She was playing with him and he couldn't blame her. From what she'd said, it didn't take a genius to figure out that truth was one of her cornerstones. "No, it's not. You want me to pour out all my secrets."

"And you can't do that. I'm not asking you for the key to your soul," she said. "I just want the truth. The real truth, not some half-lie or omission."

"Why is it so important to you?"

She shook her head. "It just is."

"You can't have it both ways, Jane. If I have to open up, then so do you."

"I . . . my ex lied to me and I promised myself I wasn't going to tolerate it from a man again."

Liam could understand that. He had some women-specific issues that for him were nonnegotiable. "Trust me—I'm not lying to you."

"But you are hiding something," she said.

They'd reached a stalemate. "Nothing important. I'm having dinner with Chase Banner and his wife tonight. He's known me more than half my life. If you are serious about wanting to get to know me, then this is a great opportunity."

"I'm not trying to be difficult."

"I know." He saw the fear deep inside her, that fear of being hurt again, and he understood that. "To be honest, I'm the same way when it comes to relationships. And I know it would be easier on both of us if I just walked out the door and didn't look back, but I don't want to."

She wrapped one arm around her waist and rubbed her finger over the base of her neck. Right where he'd kissed her earlier.

"What time?"

"In about an hour," he said, glancing down at his watch. "There are parts of my life that I don't share with anyone."

She nodded. "I've never learned to do that. I see everyone as a new friend and am always disappointed when I'm proven wrong."

"Give me a chance, Jane," he said, realizing that he really wanted her to.

"Okay. Where should I meet you for dinner?"

"The lobby."

"I might have to take a few calls during our date. I'm waiting on a couple."

Since he was using her as a camouflage so he could ask Chase and Wendy questions, he didn't think he could quibble. But the next time they had dinner, her phone was staying in her room. "You can keep the phone on during dinner but afterwards, it goes off."

"Umm, why?"

"Because I'm going to get serious about teaching you to be a bad girl. And answering a work phone call isn't the way to do it."

Chapter 8

Jane hadn't been on a date like this one since her ex-husband had split. Most of the men she'd gone out with had been guys she'd worked with and those dates had been casual. Not like tonight or like Liam. Everything with him felt more intense.

She wanted to take her time getting dressed, fixing her hair and makeup so that tonight if she decided to ask Liam up to her room, he'd be unable to resist her.

But her knowledge of makeup and hair only went so far, so she text-messaged Shanna and asked her to come to her room.

"I can't believe you are really going to let me do this," Shanna said.

Jane looked at her friend in the mirror. "It's about time."

"I agree. Why tonight?"

"I have a date."

"With one of the casino guys or someone new?"

"Liam," she said.

"Is tonight the night you leave old Jane behind?" Shanna asked as she artfully applied makeup to Jane's face.

"Now I wish I'd never mentioned that to you."

"I was just teasing. You make it sound like you're transforming yourself."

She glanced up, looking at her friend in the mirror. "Aren't I?"

Shanna shook her head. She put her makeup brushes down and picked up the flat iron. She met Jane's eyes in the mirror.

"No. You're exploring the parts of you that you've always ignored."

Jane liked the sound of that way better than she did thinking of herself as a bad girl. There was a part of her that didn't want to be bad. Even now, she was struggling with things she knew a rule-breaker would do.

Shanna used the flat iron to put random long curls into her chin-length hair. Then she had Jane bend over and tousle it. When Shanna was finished with her hair and makeup and Jane looked in the mirror, she was surprised at what she saw.

"Wow, you look good, Jane."

She did. For once, even her internal critic was silent about her looks. She modeled two different outfits for Shanna and finally decided on a tight-fitting black shirt that came to a deep vee between her breasts and a calf-length, camel-colored skirt that was deceptively conservative. The slit in the side went all the way to her thigh.

"Go get 'em, Janie."

She hugged her friend good-bye as she left. Jane took one more moment to check her BlackBerry and follow-up on one e-mail she'd received regarding the road trip. She had several media representatives meeting the guys once they arrived here in Vegas. And T.J. was e-mailing her updates of where they were.

She left her room without a backward glance, feeling more powerful and feminine than she ever had before. And the source of that emotion came from deep inside her. She realized that somehow she'd let Rodney steal that from her.

The piped-in music in the hallways was Vivaldi, and as she

walked to the elevator the living melody of "Spring" played loudly in her mind. She thought of renewal and growth, and knew it was past time for her to stop being so mired in the past.

Not anymore, she thought, remembering her new look that Shanna had helped her create.

Tears stung the back of her eyes and she blinked several times to clear them.

The elevator car arrived. She stepped inside, grateful to see it was empty. The richly paneled car had mirrors on the back wall. She forced herself to stare at her own reflection, trying to objectively see a woman who was confident and sexy, but her smile looked forced and her eyes way too serious for a woman in Vegas.

The fact that she had almost made the adjustments needed in her internal thinking to match the woman she saw reflected should have made her smile more relaxed.

The doors opened at the lobby but she couldn't make herself get off until she glanced up and saw the same loser she'd always been. The one who'd completely ignored the fact that her husband was cheating on her.

She squared her shoulders and stepped onto the marble floor that led to the lobby. Liam was there, already talking to one of the men he'd been gambling with last night.

He waved her over. She took her time, imitating Shanna's walk. She was conscious of the sway of her hips and the brush of her skirt against her legs. She kept her gaze firmly locked on Liam and saw his eyes drift down her body.

"Jane, this is Bradley Jameson. Bradley, this is Jane Monte."

"It's a pleasure to meet you, Jane."

"You, too."

"Are you Liam's lady luck?" Jameson asked.

"Am I?" she asked Liam.

He wrapped one arm around her waist, drawing her into

the curve of his body. He put his hand under her chin, tipping her head back as he lowered his mouth and kissed her. The kiss wasn't a simple hello, it was a claim. His mouth moved over hers and she let him dominate the embrace. After long minutes had passed, he lifted his head, rubbing his thumb over her lower lip.

She liked the feel of his hand against her face. He made her feel cherished and beautiful, two things she could safely say she'd never experienced before. But that didn't mean she knew how to handle it, or him. That she even wanted to.

"Yeah, Jane's my lucky charm," Liam said.

Liam couldn't take his eyes off of Jane or get his mind off of anything other than holding her in his arms, so it was probably a good thing that he'd already asked Jameson the questions he had for him. Once again, lust had short-circuited his brain.

"Where are we meeting your friends?" she asked when they got in the taxi line in front of the hotel.

"The Aureole—have you eaten there?"

"No. I've never even heard of it. I did eat at Le Cirque over at the Bellagio. I'm not really much of a foodie," she said.

"Me, either. I was excited to find a Krispy Kreme at the Venetian."

She laughed. "I don't get the Krispy Kreme phenomenon."

He shrugged. "I'm from Florida so they aren't a new thing to me. I grew up eating hot donuts at the fire station with my dad."

"You're close to him, aren't you?"

"As close as he lets anyone be."

"What about your mom? Did she and your sister team up against all you boys . . . how many brothers did you say you had?"

"Three," he said. "I have three brothers."

They moved forward in the cab line, but Liam was trapped in the past. Trapped in those long-ago memories of his mother. Andi, his baby sister, had never had a chance to know their mom, Bridget.

"So did they?"

"No. My mom died when Andi was a baby."

"Oh. I'm sorry."

He shook his head. "It was a long time ago."

She put her arm around his waist, hugging him close for a moment. He wrapped his arms around her and held her when she would have moved back. No one had ever offered him comfort over the loss of his mother.

His dad had been too busy grieving, and besides, boys didn't cry. His father had never said those words but he hadn't needed to. And as a six-year-old boy with his parental world narrowed to just the old man, Liam had made sure he was someone his father would be proud of.

They had to move forward in the taxi line, but he kept his arm around Jane's shoulder while he told the bellman where they were going. Jane entered the cab first, sliding across the seat. The slit in her skirt parted and her long, slim leg was revealed. He sat down next to her, putting his hand on the skin displayed.

"You have pretty legs," he said, running his finger down the edge of the fabric. She shivered under his touch.

"At home I try to run three miles every morning."

"I'm a runner, too."

"More than three miles?" she asked, the hint of doubt in her voice at odds with the sexy, confident woman he knew her to be.

"Yeah, but I'm a lot bigger than you and I have that donut addiction."

She laughed, pulling the edge of her skirt over her exposed leg. He wanted to push the fabric back and look his fill. In fact, he wished they were out of this cab and somewhere private where he could push the skirt up to her waist; he was dying to touch her and taste her. God, less than twenty-four hours ago he'd been able to resist her, and now all he could think about was making her his.

"Liam?"

"Yeah?" Her legs were long and lean and her body was slim but curvy. Images of her from this afternoon when she'd been sprawled on that lounge chair wearing nothing but a brief bikini flashed through his mind. Only this time he was sitting next to her.

"You're staring at me," she said with a nervous little laugh.

"How am I staring at you?"

"Like you're hungry."

He was, he thought. A growl left his throat without his permission.

She laughed again. "I thought you didn't do the casual-sex thing."

"I don't."

There was nothing casual about what he felt for Jane. He wasn't the kind of guy to examine his feelings and he didn't now, but he knew there was something totally different about this woman and her effect on him. If he was a smarter man, he'd probably walk away from her.

But he liked danger. He liked walking on the edge between safety and peril and there was no way in hell he was walking away again.

"That's not a very Vegas-like attitude," she said.

"I'm not from Vegas and neither are you."

"This isn't real," she said, her tone low as if she were really talking to herself.

He pushed the fabric of her skirt aside and ran his finger up the inside of her thigh. She put her hand on his wrist but didn't push him away. "You feel real to me."

SEX WITH A STRANGER / 91

"That's not what I meant," she said. "This is going to be a total buzz kill, but I need to define what's happening between us."

He turned his hand in her grip and folded his fingers over hers. She had long fingers but her hand seemed small and fragile in his.

"Define it how?"

She nibbled on her lower lip, completely wiping away the rest of her lip gloss. "Uh . . . vacation fling."

Liam leaned back in the seat next to her. He'd had those before and every instinct in his body said that *temporary lover* wasn't the role he wanted to play in Jane's life. But what else did he have to offer her? He wasn't the settling-down kind and they lived on opposite coasts.

He knew her suggestion was the best of both worlds. "How long will you be in Vegas?"

"Ten more days."

He wasn't going to say no. Hell, he'd been in a state of semiarousal since he'd kissed her in the hallway outside her room.

"Are you sure?" he asked, because he knew she was struggling with defining herself and no matter what else happened between them—even just a temporary affair—he didn't want to be responsible for hurting her.

She nodded.

"Then I'm your man."

Wendy and Chase Banner were the perfect hosts as they led her and Liam through the Aureole. The restaurant was exquisite. There were floor-to-ceiling, climate-controlled wine racks. Two women dressed in catsuits called "wine angels" were lifted via a harness to retrieve whatever vintage was requested.

"As you probably can guess, the wine list here is really extensive. They have a sampling menu that's pretty good if you want to try more than one wine," Wendy said as they were seated.

Jane's limited knowledge of wine wasn't good enough for her to feel comfortable ordering from the wine list so the sampling menu would probably be a good choice for her. She expected Liam to seem out of place here but he blended in easily, making her realize what a chameleon the man could be.

"Sounds like a great choice," Jane said.

"It is," Liam agreed. "The chef here is one of the best in the world."

She gave him a quick glance from under her lashes. "Better than the Krispy Kreme man?"

Liam laughed, taking her hand in his. "That's like comparing apples and oranges."

She smiled at him and turned back to her menu. He kept their hands joined and resting on his leg under the table.

The men were talking about an upcoming poker tournament that was to be held in the Royal Banner in a week's time. Jane decided she'd definitely get the tasting menu with the wine selections already made for her.

Wendy Banner had the kind of patrician looks that Jane associated with New England conservatism and generations of inherited wealth. There was something familiar about her face.

"Do you gamble?" Jane asked Wendy.

"Not really. I spend some time in the casino when Chase has business associates that he needs to entertain, but it's not really my thing."

"What is your thing?" Jane asked. Liam had mentioned earlier that Wendy was a stay-at-home mom. All of her friends worked, even those with kids, so she was curious what that life would be like.

"Tennis, shopping, and making sure the next generation of Banners lives up to the expectations of her family back east," Chase said from across the table.

His tone was light but Wendy narrowed her eyes. "I do like to play tennis—my team won the last tournament held at the club. Do you play?"

"No. I'm not really that athletic," Jane said. "But I do go shopping."

Thinking of all the time she'd spent in malls and high-end retail shops retooling her attire to fit her new image, she was a little burned-out on shopping especially since she'd never really been into it. But she'd felt a need to at least pretend she had something in common with Wendy.

"Wendy lives to shop," Chase said.

"That's not entirely true, but if you are looking for someone to go shopping with while you're here, give me a ring. I just got back from a trip to Manhattan to purchase my Spring wardrobe."

"Wendy's main goal in life is to spend money faster than I can make it," Chase said.

"Not true. My mom and sister and I always go to New York in February to check out the new trends."

"Are you close?" Jane asked. Wendy seemed like someone who had it all. She was lithe and fashionably dressed, had a gorgeous husband and kids.

"Yes, we are. I took our daughters with me this time. Chase was going to join us but with all the stuff going on at the casino, he couldn't make it."

"Do you mean the fire?" Jane asked.

"There's actually been three fires," Chase said.

"All at the Royal Banner?"

"No. The first one was at C&H."

"I didn't realize there had been more than one fire. Were they deliberately set?"

"We think so," Chase said. "But so far the investigators haven't figured out who is setting them."

"Fire investigations take time," Liam said.

"How much time?" Jane asked.

"Depends on the arsonist," Liam said. "Did Gracie and Ashley enjoy their trip to New York?"

Wendy nodded. "They had a great time. They got to meet Mary Kate and Ashley Olsen at one of the fashion shows, which was the highlight as far as they were concerned."

"How old are they?" Jane asked. From having been part of a married couple for five years and having socialized with other married types, she knew that once people had kids, they loved to talk about them.

"Gracie is ten and Ashley is eight," she said. She reached into her handbag and took out her cell phone. "Here's a photo of them."

She handed her phone to Jane and she saw two girls that looked a lot like Wendy standing in Rockefeller Plaza. They had Chase's eyes, she thought. She felt a pang.

"Let me see," Liam said. "I haven't seen the girls in two years."

"If you ever pulled yourself away from the casino, you could."

"We need him to stay in the casino and play, dear. That's what makes us so successful."

"That's true," Liam said. "And I haven't had a lot of time."

They ordered their dinner and enjoyed a leisurely meal. Once the talk turned away from the casino and Chase's work, all the tension dissipated between the other couple.

There was an underlying tension between her and Liam but it was more sexual in nature. He kept her hand in his whenever possible. He touched her constantly, whether it was to share a bit of his salmon or to brush her hair off her cheek. She tried to remember this was just a vacation fling but being with Wendy and Chase made her feel more grounded in the real world. And she knew that this was a mistake. Knew that she had to be very careful not to let herself be deluded into thinking that Liam was hers for longer than ten days.

Chapter 9

Jane excused herself from the table to take a call from Josef. The guys had a flat tire and were delayed in some little town that had very poor cell reception.

"I'll let everyone on my end know that they'll be delayed arriving here. Are they staying in character?"

"Yes. T.J. sounded like some Boston street kid when I talked to him."

"Good. I'll start writing a press release to include the tire incident."

"I'm at dinner now so e-mail it to me when you have it finished," Josef said.

"No problem."

Jane hung up and then looked around for someplace quiet to do the write-up. She finally settled into a corner at the end of the hallway leading to the bathrooms. She wrote as quickly as she could, using only her thumbs on the small BlackBerry keyboard.

"What are you doing?"

Liam startled her and she almost dropped her BlackBerry. She glanced up. His features were tight, and he put his hands on his hips while he stood there. Backlit from the restaurant, she couldn't make out his expression. Was he angry or worried about her?

"I have to write a quick release. I'll be back to the table in a few minutes."

"Wendy and Chase have to leave. Their sitter just called and Gracie is running a fever."

"Oh, I'm sorry to hear that," Jane said, her mind still on the text she was composing in her mind. "Let me finish this sentence up and I'll come back and say good-bye to them."

"I'll do it for you. Finish your work so we can enjoy the rest of our date."

She started to apologize for working but stopped herself. This was who she was and Liam would have to take her as she was because she wasn't changing for any man.

"I'll be back."

She nodded and finished typing the press release. She sent it to Josef and her staff before leaving the hallway. Liam sat alone at their table.

He stood up when she returned. "Are you done?"

"For now. I'm probably going to have to write at least one more release before the night is over."

"I want this night for us," he said.

"Me, too. It won't be that distracting. Did you order dessert?"

"No. I figured we'd pick up something later."

"What's this about?" she asked. "I'm not going to apologize for working tonight."

He leaned across the table to take one of her hands in his. "I'm not asking you to."

"You seem like you are," she said. Normally she would have let this go, but knowing that this was temporary freed her in a way she hadn't expected it to. She didn't have to pretend to be all nicey-nice with him because their affair had an end-date.

He shrugged. "I don't like you being distracted from me."

"Distracted from you? Do you have any idea how that

sounds?" After her divorce she'd wondered if maybe Rodney had strayed because she'd been very involved in her job. Was it because he wasn't the main focus of her life that he'd gotten bored in their relationship and looked elsewhere? She had no idea because she'd never been able to talk to Rodney. Having cleaned out their bank account and disappeared to Aruba, he hadn't come back to the States to divorce her. Everything had been handled via their attorneys.

"Hell, yes. Like I'm some kind of Neanderthal who has no concept of what a modern woman is like."

Memories of Rodney disappeared. Liam was the kind of man who could easily dominate her entire life if she let him. And part of her wanted that. She wanted to get to the point where she could stop thinking about who she was. She bit her lip to keep from smiling. "Well, is that who you really are?"

"Yes. Don't let this fool you," he said, gesturing to his clothing and the environment which she had already observed that he fit easily into.

"So you really are a me-Tarzan, you-Jane kind of guy?" she asked. That type had never been attracted to her. Liam had no idea how different this entire experience was for her and how hard she was working to keep her cool and stay one step ahead of him.

"Yeah, I am. I try not to let it show too much but sometimes I can't help myself," he said. "My sister would kick my ass if she heard me saying this."

"She sounds a lot like you," she said, because she detected how much it bothered Liam to be experiencing jealousy over her job.

He shrugged and signed the check.

"I can't imagine that's very conducive to long-term relationships," she said.

"Depends on the woman," he said. "Some women like to be taken care of."

"But that wouldn't appeal to you," she said. "You want a woman who's as strong as you are."

"True. Doesn't mean that it's not nice to once in a while be with a woman who just wants to make me happy."

"I don't want you not to be happy."

"Yeah, I didn't mean it that way."

"My days of living for a guy are over," she said.

"I can't imagine you ever living for someone else," he said.

"I didn't exactly live for my ex-husband but I really tried to be what he wanted."

She glanced up at him and noticed that he was watching her. She liked having his complete attention.

"What did he want?"

"I have no idea. In the end I don't think he did, either. But then I think most people don't know what they want."

"Some people," he said.

But not Liam. He wasn't about subtlety and there was a part of her that liked that about him. She felt like she could trust him but then remembered he was hiding something from her.

The electronic beat pulsed through the club and though Liam wanted to be alone with Jane, he was enjoying dancing with her too much to leave. Plus, here on the dance floor she didn't have her BlackBerry in her hand.

He kept one hand on her hip as they gyrated together on the dance floor to the Shakira song "Hips Don't Lie."

"I love this song," Jane said, leaning into him and speaking directly in his ear to be heard over the music.

He'd never cared for it particularly. He liked the video, but then it was hard not to like looking at Shakira.

She was moving tentatively, very conscious of the swaying bodies around them.

"Show me how much you like it," he said.

"How?"

"Dance for me."

"Dance for you?"

He quirked one eyebrow at her, stroking his finger down the side of her neck. She shivered as he rubbed the pad of his finger over her pulse.

"Okay."

She let go of him and danced around him, her hips finding the beat, and Liam knew he was trapped. Just like when he was in a burning building, almost out of oxygen but unable to leave, neither could he pull away from Jane.

He drew her to him, bent his head to capture her lips. They kept moving in time with the music but it was more the swaying of one being than two. He held her close, stroking his hands from her waist to her hips.

Her mouth opened under his and he felt her tongue against his own.

Her mouth opened under his and he told himself to take it slow, but slow wasn't in his programming with this woman. She was pure feminine temptation and he had her in his arms. He slid his hands down her back, wishing he could push his hands up under her shirt. The elegant line of her back tempted him. He wanted to feel her flesh under his hands, to explore every part of her.

Her bodice clung to the curves of her breasts. He turned her in his arms, drawing her back against his chest. He put one hand low on her waist to hold them together while he swiveled their hips. She lifted one of her arms and wrapped it around his neck. The material of her blouse shifted and he watched a bead of sweat travel down the snowy white curves.

"If we were alone right now," he said into her ear, "I'd trace this with my tongue."

He fingered the edge of her blouse, tracing the deep vee and the fleshy globes of her breasts. He knew he had to stop but it was hard to do. No one was paying the least bit of attention to them but he wasn't into exhibitionism.

He made himself let go of her. She danced away from him a few steps, twirled and came back. She teased him with feather-light caresses on his neck and chest. She danced around behind him and he felt her touch on his shoulder—her fingers drifted down his back.

Liam had never seen anything more beautiful than this woman in his arms. She was so responsive to his touch and he wanted more. It fed the fire that had started earlier in the cab. No, that wasn't true. This fire had started when he'd come back out of the thirty-fifth-floor hallway and found that she'd waited for him.

Found that she'd fought her way past her own panic and fear to wait for him. His skin felt too tight. He tried to get back to the lust-only place he'd been just moments before but it was too late for that. What he wanted from Jane was more than sex and he wanted her now. If he didn't take her soon he was going to self-combust.

The words swirled around in his head. He'd wanted her, but until this moment, he hadn't realized how fiercely.

He ran his hands slowly down the side of her body, afraid to believe she was really his. Temporarily, he reminded himself.

He firmly pushed those thoughts out of his head. She stared up at him, her eyes heavy-lidded with desire. Her lips were swollen from his kisses and there was a flush to her skin that he suspected was caused by arousal.

She had one hand on his chest, keeping just a small distance between them. There was something very fragile inside this ultracompetent and professional woman. He pulled her more fully into his arms, cradling her to his chest with one arm. She closed her eyes and buried her face in his neck as the tempo of the music changed to something slow and sultry. Each exhalation went through him.

He was so hard and hot for her that he knew he might come, but he was determined to wait. Then he felt the minute touches of her tongue against his neck.

She moaned a sweet sound that he leaned down to capture in his mouth. She tipped her head to the side immediately, allowing him access to her mouth. She held his shoulders, undulating against him, rubbing her center over his erection.

God, he hadn't been this hot since he'd been a teenager. He scraped his fingernail over her nipple and she shivered in his arms. He pushed her back a little so he could see her. Her nipples distended, pushing against the fabric of her blouse and begging for his mouth.

"Let's get out of here."

Her eyes widened and she nodded, taking his hand in hers and leading him off the dance floor. They paused at the table to pick up her purse and his jacket and then left the club. The music faded as they moved away.

The night air was cool and refreshing after the heat of the club and the woman he'd held in his arms. He draped his jacket over her shoulders and led her toward their hotel.

Jane expected the sensual web that had engulfed them to be shattered when they walked back to the room. But it wasn't. Liam kept his arm around her, and though he didn't rush her she felt the urgency in both of them as they made their way through the strangers crowding the sidewalk of the Vegas Strip.

It was as if a bubble enveloped her and she clung to that feeling until her doubts started trickling in. She wasn't the person this clothing and makeup advertised. She and Rodney had never made love with the lights on and their monthly sexual encounters had always been standard missionary position.

She had a feeling that Liam wasn't going to be that type

of a lover but she had no idea if she had enough knowledge to please him.

Just dancing with him had already aroused her more than anything she'd ever done with her husband. While she had some minor, pleasant-feeling orgasms with Rodney, they were the exception rather than the rule.

They entered the lobby of the Royal Banner and the lights seemed too bright after the ones that filtered through the inky darkness of the sidewalk outside the hotel. Her steps slowed until she almost stopped.

"Baby?"

No man had ever called her by an endearment, not even her father. She was just too sensible for nicknames . . . only Shanna called her Janie and she had a feeling that was to make her lighten up.

"I'm not what you might be expecting," she said.

He arched one eyebrow at her. "What do you think I'm expecting?"

"Someone who's a red-hot sex machine."

His lips twitched. "What exactly are you envisioning? I don't think I'm up to the label of red-hot sex machine, either."

She put her hands over her face. She sounded like an idiot, but she wanted to make sure he knew that she wasn't that experienced. Rodney had been her only lover. She'd waited for marriage to have sex . . .

She dropped her hands and looked up at him. "I'm making a mess of this. I just don't want you to be disappointed."

"I won't be," he said.

She wanted to argue with him but that would make her feel even more foolish than she already did. If worse came to worst, she could fake an orgasm. She'd done that a lot with Rodney.

Before she knew it they were outside the door to her room. She opened it and stepped inside. The light she'd left on over the bed created a welcoming glow.

She stood nervously inside the door, looking at the bed. Liam drew his hand down her back.

"Second thoughts?"

"No. I want to do this. It's just so . . ."

"Abrupt, now that we're alone?"

"Yes," she said, taking a deep breath. "I only ever did this with my ex-husband and I'm not sure what to do next. I think—"

His mouth settled on hers, shutting off the torrent of words. He tasted like Liam and like the wine they'd had at dinner. She put her arms around his broad shoulders and realized that this was one of those moments she'd been trying to manufacture. A moment that would definitely put her in new territory for the woman she wanted to become.

Was that why she was so nervous? She was going to have sex with her temporary lover, with a man who was nothing but her vacation fling.

But this was what she wanted. Where she wanted to be. Funny to have a moment of clarity while her body was on fire for this man. She had longed for this moment to be draped in magic, but she knew now that she wanted to feel every moment of it, to enjoy this change she'd forced herself to make. She drew back and smiled up at him.

"Better?"

"Yes, much. Thanks, Liam."

"No problem. Will you do me a favor?"

She nodded.

"Do you still have that negligee you were wearing when we met?"

"Ah, yes."

"Will you put it on for me?"

She nodded. "I'll be right back."

She went into the bathroom where she'd left the garment hanging on the hook on the back of the door. She looked at herself in the mirror. Her skin was flushed and a streak of excitement pulsed through her. She kicked off her shoes and slowly removed her skirt, then pulled her shirt over her head and made herself slow down.

She didn't want Liam to think she was . . . what? She'd already showed him that scary, needy side of herself. No more, she thought. It was time to take control.

She'd read enough copies of *Cosmopolitan* magazine to know that there were sex moves that would make him crazy for her. She'd read them hoping to spice things up with her ex but he'd never been interested. She took her time putting on the negligee.

She reapplied her lipstick and stared into the mirror, remembering the way she'd felt in the club when the music had been beating wildly around them and pulsing through her own body. She tried to recapture a little bit of that.

She let the sounds of that Shakira song play through her mind. She moved her hips in time to the music playing in her head and remembered the way Liam's eyes had narrowed when she'd danced around him. Remembered the feel of his erection pressed against her belly as he'd held her close.

She took a deep breath and opened the bathroom door, stepping out into the room. Liam was lying on the bed. He'd removed his shirt, belt, socks and shoes. There was a tattoo of a four-leaf clover on his left pectoral. He had the pillows piled up behind him.

He was in some seriously good shape. His chest was heavy with muscles and he had a six-pack abdomen. There was no hair on his chest.

She couldn't stop looking at him. She took a deep breath and found her courage and strength in the woman she was dying to become. Then she walked out of the shadows and stood at the foot of the bed.

Liam sat up straighter. "Come here."

Chapter 10

Liam loved Jane's cream-colored, sheer negligee. He'd had a few inconvenient fantasies about that nightgown over the last few days. He sank deeper into the pillows, watching her as she walked toward him.

She moved like she had earlier this evening in the lobby—all easy, long-limbed grace. Each step was slowly measured. Her shoulders were back and her hips moving sensuously.

Blood rushed through his veins, pooling in his center. A smile of intent spread over his face.

"Finally, I get the chance to explore your pleasure," he said.

"And yours," she countered.

She sank down next to him on the bed, a hint of shyness still in her eyes. "Climb up here."

"Not yet."

He arched one eyebrow at her. "Do you have something else in mind?"

"Yes. Can I . . . just lie there and let me . . ."

He growled deep in his throat when she leaned forward to brush kisses against his chest. Her lips were sweet and not shy as she explored his torso, tracing his tattoo over and over again. The tattoo was his lucky charm. He'd gotten it when he was fourteen—the old man had pitched a fit about it but eventually had let it go.

As Jane leaned down over his chest he felt the brush of her hair against his skin and then the edge of her teeth as she nibbled at his pecs.

He watched her, his eyes narrowing and his pants feeling damned uncomfortable. Her tongue darted out and brushed against his nipple. He arched off the bed and put his hand on the back of her head, urging her to stay where she was.

She put her hands on his shoulders and eased her way down his chest, tracing each of the muscles that ribbed his abdomen, then slowly made her way lower. He could feel his heartbeat in his erection and he knew he was going to lose it if he didn't take control.

But another part of him wanted to just sit back and let her have her way with him. When she reached the edge of his pants, she stopped and glanced up his body to his face.

Her hand went to his erection, brushing over his straining length. "I guess you like that."

"Hell, yeah," he said, pulling her to him. He lifted her slightly so that her nipples brushed his chest.

"Now it's my turn," he said.

She nibbled on her lips as he rotated his shoulders so that his chest rubbed against her breasts.

"I like *that*," she said.

Blood roared in his ears. He was so hard, so full right now that he needed to be inside of her body.

Impatient with the fabric of her negligee, he shoved it up and out of his way, then caressed her creamy thighs. God, she was soft. She moaned as he neared her center and then sighed when he brushed his fingertips across the crotch of her panties.

The cotton was warm and wet. He slipped one finger under the material and hesitated for a second, looking down into her eyes.

Her eyes were heavy-lidded. She bit down on her lower

lip and he felt the minute movements of her hips as she tried to move his touch where she needed it.

He was beyond teasing her or prolonging anything. He ripped her panties aside, plunging two fingers into her humid body. She squirmed against him.

He pulled her head down to his so he could taste her. Her mouth opened over his and he told himself to take it slow, but slow wasn't possible with this woman.

He nibbled on her and held her at his mercy. Her nails dug into his shoulders and she leaned up, brushing against his chest. Her nipples were hard points, and he pulled away from her mouth, glancing down to see them pushing against his chest.

He caressed her back and spine, scraping his nail down the length of it. He followed the line of her back down the indentation above her backside.

She closed her eyes and held her breath as he fondled her, running his finger over her nipple. It was velvety compared to the satin smoothness of her breast. He brushed his finger back and forth until she bit her lower lip and shifted on his lap. He wanted to give her this pleasure because from the few things she said, he'd guessed that her marriage hadn't been that great in bed or out.

And seeing the sexy, confident woman she was disappear when they'd neared the bedroom had made him want to find her ex and beat the crap out of him. Women were vulnerable when it came to sex. Not in just a physical way but in an emotional one as well, and Liam made it a point to make sure that his lovers knew he found them sexy and beautiful.

She moaned a sweet sound that he leaned up to capture in his mouth. She tipped her head to the side immediately, allowing him access. She held his shoulders and moved on him, rubbing her center over his erection.

He pushed her back a little bit so he could see her. Her breasts were bare, nipples distended and begging for his mouth. He lowered his head and suckled.

He held her still with a hand on the small of her back. He buried his other hand in her hair and arched her over his arm. Both of her breasts were thrust up at him. He had a lap full of woman and he knew that he wanted Jane more than he'd wanted any woman in a long time.

She made the fires he was always fighting seem tame. Nothing compared to the way she made him feel.

Her eyes were closed, her hips moving subtly against him, and when he blew on her nipple he saw gooseflesh spread down her body.

He loved the way she reacted to his mouth on her breasts. Her nipples were so sensitive he was pretty sure he could bring her to an orgasm just from touching her there.

The globes were full and fleshy, more than a handful. He hardened as he wondered what his cock would feel like thrust between them.

He leaned down and licked the valley between her breasts, imagining his cock sliding back and forth there. He'd swell and she'd moan his name watching him.

He bit carefully at the lily-white skin of her chest, suckling at her so that he'd leave his mark. He wanted her to remember this moment and what they had done when she was alone later.

He kept kissing and rubbing, pinching her nipples until her hands clenched in his hair and she rocked her hips harder against his length. He lifted his hips, thrusting up against her. He bit down carefully on her tender, aroused nipple. She screamed his name and he hurriedly covered her mouth with his, wanting to feel every bit of her passion.

He rocked her until the storm passed and she quieted in his arms. He held her close, her bare breasts brushing against his chest. He was so hard he thought he'd die if he didn't get inside her.

He glanced down at her and saw she was watching him. The fire in her eyes made his entire body tight with anticipation.

His EMT training refused to let him have sex without asking about her history, but that could break the mood so he just reached for the condom he'd put in his pocket earlier. Actually, he'd optimistically put a handful in there. He put the condom on one-handed and turned back to her.

"Hurry," she said, no shadows in her eyes now. He loved that he'd banished the painful memories that her ex-husband had left her with.

"Not a chance. I'm going to savor you."

"I don't know how long I can last," she said. "I really want you. Come to me now."

Shifting off his lap, she settled next to him on the bed. She opened her arms and her legs, inviting him into her body, and he went. He lowered himself over her and rubbed against her, shifting until he'd caressed every part of her.

She reached between his legs and fondled his sac, cupping him in her hands, and he shuddered. He needed to be inside her now. He shifted and lifted her thighs, wrapping her legs around his waist. Her hands fluttered between them and their eyes met.

He held her hips steady and entered her slowly, thrusting deeply until he was fully seated. Her eyes widened with each inch he gave her. She clutched at his hips as he started thrusting, holding him to her, eyes half closed and her head tipped back.

He leaned down and caught one of her nipples in his teeth, scraping very gently. She started to tighten around him, her hips moving faster, demanding more, but he kept the pace slow, steady, wanting her to come before he did.

He suckled her nipple and rotated his hips to catch her pleasure point with each thrust and he felt her hands in his hair clenching as she threw her head back and her climax ripped through her.

He varied his thrusts, finding a rhythm that would draw out the tension at the base of his spine. Something that would make his time in her body, wrapped in her silky limbs, last forever.

He leaned back on his haunches and tipped her hips up to give him deeper access to her body. Then she scraped her nails down his back, clutched his buttocks, and drew him in. His sac tightened and his blood roared in his ears as he felt everything in his world center on this one woman.

He called her name as he came and hoped she'd sleep now, because if she didn't he was going to curl himself around her and tell her all his secrets. She'd brought him completely out of himself and into a spot where he'd never thought he'd be—a place of vulnerability that he'd hoped never to find.

The sweat dried on their bodies as Liam held her in his arms. He didn't say anything and she didn't want to talk, either. She'd never experienced anything like that. Faking it hadn't been necessary. In fact, she doubted she could have faked anything that would be believable now that he'd made love to her.

He rolled to his side, holding her loosely while one of his hands caressed her. He made slow, languid sweeps with his hand from the curve of her waist up to her breast and then back down again.

She kept her gaze on the bottom of his jaw, not letting herself look any higher than that. She wasn't sure what would happen next. A vacation fling sounded thrilling and fun in theory but now that she was here in bed with Liam, she had no idea what to do next.

"You're tensing up," he said.

"Sorry."

She tried to force herself to relax but now that her mind had started going in that direction she couldn't shake it off that track.

"What are you worrying about?"

"Um . . . nothing."

"Liar."

"That's not really nice."

"I'm not a nice guy."

"Now who's lying?"

"You think I'm nice," he said, making it a statement.

"Sometimes."

He smacked her lightly on the butt. "I don't really think of myself like that. *Nice* always sounds like a pansy."

"Pansy? Liam, you're one of the most masculine men I've ever met. I can't imagine anyone thinking of you in those terms."

"No one does," he said, rolling back over on top of her. He settled his body over hers. Braced on his elbows, his erection nestled between her legs. He caressed the side of her face with one finger. "You just keep thinking of me as a stud and we'll be okay."

She shook her head. "Stud?"

"You can admit it," he said.

"I guess so."

"Do I have to prove it again?"

She shook her head. She was out of her element here but it was clear that Liam was comfortable. Teasing her, holding her. He was just relaxed and being himself, and she wished that she could find the same comfort, promising herself that one day soon she'd be able to.

"I don't think I've ever called anyone a stud. It sounds almost as silly as *pansy*."

"Are you making fun of me?"

"Never," she said. "It's just that I'm used to being a good girl. You know, saying the right thing all the time. Acting a certain way."

He leaned down and kissed her. "You're a bad girl in the making, remember?"

With his naked erection at the portal of her body, it took a second for her to understand what she was asking. She wished he'd thrust into her and stop talking.

He leaned down and kissed her so tenderly before moving away to put on a condom, then came back down on top of her. He bent down to capture the tip of her breast in his mouth. He sucked her deep in his mouth, his teeth lightly scraping against her sensitive flesh. His other hand played at her other breast, arousing her, making her arch against him in need.

"Now, Liam. I can't wait."

"But I'm not ready yet."

She reached between them and took his erection in her hand, bringing him closer to her, spreading her legs wider so she was totally open to him. "Show me what you're made of, Stud."

He lifted his head, the tips of her breasts damp from his mouth and very tight. He rubbed his chest over them before sliding deep into her body.

She wanted to close her eyes as he made love to her. To somehow keep him from seeing how susceptible she was to him, but then she knew that no matter what she hid from him she wouldn't be able to hide from herself. She didn't know if she was ever going to be "bad" enough to feel comfortable making love with a man and not letting her emotions get involved.

She slid her hands down his back, cupping his butt as he thrust deeper into her. Their eyes met; staring deep into his eyes made her feel like this was more than a temporary affair. She knew that was an illusion, that what Liam and she had was temporary. The chimera of what Vegas had to offer.

But when she wrapped her legs around his waist as he pounded into her, driving them both toward release, she refused to think anymore. Emotions swamped her and she felt everything more intensely. His hot erection between her legs. His hard hands rubbing over her breasts. His warm mouth on the side of her neck. The cotton hotel sheets under her back and how the rhythm of his thrusting moved her on the bed.

She felt her body start to tighten around him, catching her by surprise. She climaxed before he did. He gripped her hips, holding her down and thrusting into her two more times before he came with a loud grunt, then called her name.

He held her afterwards, both of them looking into each other's eyes—the lightness he'd brought to them earlier had disappeared. She had the feeling that Liam wasn't feeling too nice at the moment. There was a serious intensity in those midnight eyes of his.

She wanted to close her eyes to break the moment, but at the same time was afraid to. Afraid to look away or let go, because she knew this wasn't going to last. Something indefinable passed between them and she shivered a little. He held her so close she could barely breathe. Then, all of a sudden, he let her go.

He moved away after a few moments, pushing to his feet to head for the bathroom. She lay on the bed, staring after him and knowing that she had to toughen up. Had to keep up the façade of the new Jane.

New-rule-breaking Jane who wasn't about to fall in love with a man who was only a vacation fling.

Security had been tighter tonight—when he tried to get a key to a room, he'd almost been caught. But then he hung out in this casino enough that he'd been able to play it off.

But his pulse was still racing and he hated that. It made him feel like a junkie who needed a hit ... hell, he did need a hit. He needed to find a place to start the fire.

But then he found the perfect solution in the wedding chapel. Statistics said most of those poor fools weren't going to be in it for the long haul. And Chase prided himself on the sophisticated weddings he offered at the C&H. He'd even married his own wife there to encourage business.

Everything Chase did was for the good of the casinos, which gave him an extra little rush as he stood in the small room behind the wedding chapel reserved for the officiate of the ceremony.

The rags worked well last time but he knew he couldn't use the same materials each time—not if he wanted to keep the arson investigators from figuring out who he was. He didn't like that woman investigator. She was always nosing around and asking questions. He'd managed to avoid her so far, but it was only a matter of time before they would want to interview him.

Being new to the arson business, he'd had to go online to find something new to start the fire with this time. He couldn't keep filling up his gas can at different stations around the city.

He took out the three cans of lighter fluid he'd purchased earlier in California. The drive had been a bitch but he knew he couldn't buy anything close to Vegas.

He sprayed the walls with the fluid, then the settee nestled in the corner. He used all three cans and wondered if he shouldn't have gotten a few more. He wanted the fire to smoke a lot and cause a panic.

Yeah, that would be a nice way to end the ceremony taking place next door. He pulled out his lucky lighter, flicked down on the igniter, and watched the flame.

"Hello, my friend." He wasn't sure when it had happened but he knew that the flames had become his friend.

More of a family than his real one, that was for sure. The flames always behaved the same way. Always moved and burned.

He bent down and started setting the room on fire, walking in a slow circle to ensure that everything was touched by his flame.

The fire burned hot and fierce. He panicked a little, scrambling backwards away from the flames, but he'd done a good job of dousing the entire little room with the fluid and it was going up all around him. He headed for the door as thick smoke and hot flames took over, sucking the oxygen from the room. He opened the door to the staff hallway and ran away from the burning room. When he got to the kitchen, one of the dishwashers saw him but he didn't make eye contact and just kept walking out into the night.

The further away he got from the blaze, the better he felt about it. Yeah, he'd done it again, made big ol' Chase Banner bend to his will. A part of him hated that Chase didn't know who was responsible for the chaos at his resorts but another part of him didn't give a fuck. He liked the fact that he was getting even with Chase and the entire board of directors at Banner Casino Group.

Liam leaned over the sink and splashed water on his face, hoping to jar himself back to sensibility. He stood up and rubbed his hand over his stomach. It had been harder than he'd thought it would be to leave Jane in that bed.

He wanted to go back out there and hold her in his arms all night. To make promises he knew he couldn't keep. And demand she make similar vows to him.

"Liam?"

"Be right out."

He opened the door and found Jane standing there, wrapped in a sheet from the bed. "Your phone was ringing."

She handed it to him and moved away, walking past the

bed to stand in front of the windows. The drapes were drawn and the lights of Vegas were spread out below. She rested her forehead against the glass, staring down at something. He guessed she wasn't so much looking out the window as trying to escape him.

He checked the missed-call log and saw that he had a message from Didi. He couldn't ignore it so he dialed into his voice mail box and listened to the message.

"We've got another fire at the C&H—get over there as soon as possible." He grabbed his pants, all the while watching Jane. She stood so stiff and still, he knew this wasn't going to help matters.

"I've got to go out for a little while," he said. For the first time he really resented a blaze. This was beyond bad timing. There was no excuse he could give that wasn't going to make what just happened between them seem almost smarmy.

Her arm came up and tightened around her waist. She tucked a strand of her inky hair behind her ear and stared at him with those serious eyes of hers.

"No problem. I've got some work to do as well," she said.

"Jane—"

She held her hand up to stop him. "Don't, Liam. This is a vacation fling—no explanations needed."

But he wanted to make explanations. He hated how small and vulnerable she seemed right now. "I'm coming back later."

"I might be busy."

"Dammit—"

Her phone rang before he could say anything else. Her gaze never wavered from his face as she walked over and reached into her purse.

She glanced at the screen. "I've got to get that."

She picked up the phone and walked over to the chair, turning her back on him. He wanted to force her to put the phone down so they could finish their discussion. He knew there was no way he wasn't being painted as a villain in her mind.

But fuck it all, he knew he was in Vegas for more than a vacation and he couldn't really delay too long. He finished getting dressed, thinking about the soul sex he'd just had with this woman. He didn't want to leave until she acknowledged what had happened between them.

He walked over to the window and glanced up the Strip toward the C&H hotel. He couldn't see any big plumes of smoke, which was a bit of a relief.

He heard Jane talking in a soft voice. She jotted down notes in that confident way of hers—he had the feeling she was going to stay on the phone until he left. But he wasn't an O'Roarke for nothing. His family wrote the book on stubbornness and he could outwait her. He text-messaged Didi that he'd be over to the fire in the next forty minutes, then went and sat down in the chair next to Jane.

She covered the speaker with her thumb, tipped her head to one side, and gave him a level stare. "I'm going to be a while. You can go."

"I'll wait."

"Liam . . ."

He knew his first priority should be the fire but he wasn't leaving like this. "I'm not going until we talk. I can wait."

"Don't you have a poker seat waiting for you?" she asked caustically.

"It'll wait." His main job in the arson investigations was to go in after the fires. And he always got itchy when there was a fire and he wasn't in turn-out gear getting into the thick of things with the team.

She sighed and went back to her call. "That's all for now, Mitchell. I'll touch base later."

She hung up the phone. "What do you want to talk about?"

"Whatever's going on in your head."

"My head? I'm fine. Really. I have some work to do, and you've got to be going to wherever it is you go."

"Jane, baby, it's not as bad as you make it sound," he said. He couldn't level with her about the arson investigation but he would be as honest as he could be about what he felt for her.

"Why can't you just level with me?" she asked. She stood up, walking over to the closet and taking out a robe. She moved back into the shadows and pulled it on, dropping the sheet. He caught a glimpse of the legs before she knotted the belt at her waist.

"It's not my secret to share," he said.

"Oh. Then whose is it?"

"I can't tell you that, either."

She shook her head. "What can you tell me?"

She seemed smaller than she had before and this was exactly the reason he'd left her at the door last night. No matter who or what Jane thought she wanted to be, she wasn't cut out for casual sex. And the fact that this evening had felt anything but casual reaffirmed that.

He crossed the room, not stopping until less than an inch of space separated them. He leaned down and kissed her with all the passion and frustration that he felt. When he lifted his head, they were both breathing heavier.

"I hate like hell that I have to leave you. And I'm not going to let this keep me away."

Chapter 11

Liam made his way down one of the back streets of Vegas to the C&H. The smell of smoke grew stronger as he approached the hotel. He ran the last few blocks because he was firstly a firefighter and he needed to be on-scene where he could make a difference.

A part of him resented the fact that he'd had to stay with Jane and try to explain what was going on. Another part . . . well, let's just say he finally found a woman who made him think of something other than firefighting.

As he approached the alley he smelled rotting trash from the big Dumpster in the back and saw that the security light around the loading dock was flickering. He walked carefully to the back entrance, avoiding the puddles of waste liquid on the ground and the shards of broken glass.

A moaning sound to his left drew his attention but when he looked over there, all he saw were shadows. He kept moving toward the hotel, then heard the moan again, followed by the scraping sound of cloth against the building.

He headed toward the sound, guessing he was going to find a strung-out junkie, but knowing he couldn't afford not to investigate anyone near the fire scene.

"Anyone back there?" he asked as he approached the line of three Dumpsters.

There was a hacking cough but no other response. He

wished he had a flashlight on him but he'd come from Jane's and hadn't taken the time to get any gear.

The flickering light revealed a leg encased in dirty denim and a pair of well-worn tennis shoes. Liam reached down and shook the person.

"I don't want no trouble," the man said.

"How about a hand-out?" Liam asked. He held his hand down to the man and eventually he took it, standing up and stepping out from behind the Dumpsters.

"What's your name?"

"You can call me Joe."

"Have you been out here all night?"

The man nodded.

"Can I ask you a few questions?"

The man shrugged. "Like what?"

"You know the hotel is on fire, right?"

"I didn't set no fire."

"Did you see anyone who might have?"

"Nah. I saw something running toward the alley, but—" Joe stopped talking and shrugged. "I see him most nights."

Probably some kind of drug-induced delusion. Was he wasting his time here? "What?"

"I saw a man running through the alley," he said.

"When?"

"Right before the fire trucks arrived."

"What'd he look like?"

"Dark hair and nice clothes. You know, the kind they sell in the upscale stores at the Venetian."

"Anything else?"

Joe shook his head.

He gave the man a twenty. "If you hear anything about the fire, you can contact me at the Royal Banner. My name's Liam O'Roarke."

He entered the hotel and found a security detail waiting there. "No admittance back here."

"Who's in charge?" Liam asked the guy who wasn't letting him through.

"Paul is." The guard waved Paul over to him.

Liam held his hand out when the man approached. "I'm Liam O'Roarke—Didi Keller, the arson inspector, is expecting me."

"I'm Paul LaMar, head of security," he said, shaking Liam's hand.

"Let me check with Ms. Keller," Paul said, stepping away and speaking into his wireless headset.

Liam was glad to see that security had been brought in so quickly and that they had secured the back entrance. The casinos and lobby would be much harder to control with so many people entering and exiting.

"You're clear to go up. They are on the fifteenth floor in the wedding chapel."

"Injuries?" Liam asked.

"Four guests with smoke inhalation were treated and released."

"Was the fire contained to the wedding chapel?"

"No, some of the damage spread to the dressing rooms and hallway."

"Thanks, Paul." Liam took the stairs two at time until he got up to the fifteenth floor.

Didi was wading through the watery mess with one of the firefighters. He joined them. "Looks like the sprinklers worked this time."

"In a big way. It was enough to slow the flames and helped contain the damage."

"Liam, this is Jon. He was first on the scene."

Jon talked them through what he'd observed when he got here and then asked him a few questions. "Did you smell anything unusual when you entered the building?"

"No, sir."

"Were the doors barred to slow down your entrance into the room?" Didi asked.

He shrugged. "I had my ax out and used that."

Liam bit back a smile. His old fire team would have done the same thing. The ax was a firefighter's favorite tool.

"Did you notice anyone behaving oddly?"

"Not really. A few onlookers who wanted a closer glimpse, but Terry took care of getting them back."

"Anything else you can think of?" Didi asked.

"Seemed like a straightforward blaze. We got in and got it under control."

"Thanks, Jon."

"You want me to go talk to Terry while you deal with the wedding party?" Liam asked.

"Uh, how come I get the wedding party?"

"I can't deal with brides."

"Get a rash?" she asked.

"Yeah, something like that."

Didi drew him to the side. "No one's heard from Chase Banner tonight. That's odd."

"I had dinner with him and his wife. I think one of the kids was sick."

"You think?"

"Chase got a call from the sitter and they both left."

"You want to follow up on that?" Didi asked.

Liam nodded. "I doubt that they left dinner to come over here and start a fire."

"How's their marriage?"

"Why?"

"Maybe they don't like brides, either."

Liam shook his head. "Funny, Didi. Really funny."

The boys arrived shortly after midnight. The timing couldn't have been better, because a fight earlier in the night at the Forum had ended too soon and with a disappointing finish, so the buzz on the Strip wasn't about the boxing match. Instead it was the sight of four of Hollywood's hottest young stars driving slowly through the traffic and waving to the crowd.

Josef was pleased with the coverage Jane had gotten for them, and the articles she'd sent out had hit the AP wire. Tomorrow morning newspapers all over the country were going to be running the story.

Jane was pleased with herself and the job she'd done but felt a little hollow at the thought that this was her life. That this was the thing she'd been sacrificing for all these years.

As soon as the actors were settled into their hotel rooms, she and Mitchell started walking back to theirs.

"Late night for you, isn't it?" Mitchell asked.

"I'm not even a little sleepy. Must be that Vegas is finally getting into my system." She knew that wasn't true. Knew that she wasn't sleepy because she didn't want to go back to her room alone.

"Really? I have noticed a change in you since we've been here." Mitchell had that tone in his voice that told her he was up to no good. They'd worked together for the last three years and she liked him but he was seldom serious.

"What kind of change?" she asked.

He shrugged. "You're not so focused on work."

"I'm on vacation."

"Not anymore."

She worried that her performance may have been slipping for him to make that comment. "Tonight's event went according to plan. Josef is really happy with what we were able to pull off."

"Jane, I'm not saying you aren't still a PR dynamo, just that you seemed distracted today. Usually you would have ordered us all to a command center and micromanaged what we were doing."

But because she'd wanted to spend time with Liam, she

hadn't. "We are technically still kind of on vacation. And the guys back at the studio were in a command center."

"I know. But you weren't. It's like you finally figured out there's more to life than work."

They'd arrived back at the Royal Banner. "I'm going to hit the casinos and see if I can make enough to quit my job. Want to join me?"

"I'm not letting you quit, even if you hit the million-dollar jackpot," Jane said.

"I'm a pain in the ass. You've told me so numerous times."

"Your point is . . ."

He just laughed. "You in?"

"No," she said. She didn't want to run into Liam in the casino, and despite his vague inference that he was doing something else, she was pretty sure she'd find him sitting at a poker table.

They parted company and Jane went to the small diner that was open 24/7 and asked for a table for one. She hated eating alone. It wasn't really a good-girl rule, but she always felt super self-conscious when she sat alone in a restaurant. She'd been trying to get over that fear and tonight seemed like a good time to try again.

The diner was also a Keno club and there was a board at the back of the restaurant that had numbers flashing on it. Everywhere she went there was another chance to gamble— another risk to take.

But this felt a lot like changing her wardrobe and cutting her hair. Eating alone was another one of those small, safe changes, and tonight she needed to do something wild. Something that would convince her that she had changed, because otherwise she was going to end up back in her room, crying.

And she was way past the point where she was going to cry because of being disappointed in herself and some man.

Except she'd felt Liam's distress at leaving her. Felt how torn he'd been, and that just confused her even more.

She pulled out her phone and dialed Shanna's number. Her friend didn't answer. Jane didn't leave a message.

She left the diner before ordering anything, thinking maybe she'd hit a club or something but instead found herself standing in front of the tattoo parlor on the mezzanine level.

She watched through the window, not sure why she was fascinated by the process but knowing she was. The bald-headed man with a three-quarter-inch gauge in one ear and a day's worth of stubble on his chin glanced up at her from where he was working on a client. He had a nose ring and another one in his eyebrow—he kind of scared her because he looked so different from the people she usually saw.

She smiled at him and he smiled back. He finished up the job he was working on and she watched the entire time.

"Thinking about getting ink done?" Liam asked as he came up behind her.

He smelled like smoke but not cigarette smoke. "Maybe. You smell like fire."

"Ah, yeah, there was another one at the C&H."

"You're kidding—isn't that another one of the hotels owned by the Banners?" she asked.

"Yes, it is."

"Have you talked to Chase?"

"No. I think he's still at home with the kids."

Jane remembered the stress between Wendy and Chase and imagined tonight's incident wasn't going to help things.

"So what about it? Are you going to get a tattoo?"

She hadn't really entertained the notion of getting one. Of course, she'd never have considered it when she'd been married or even before then. But having watched the process, she was surprised to realize she was considering it.

"Maybe. I haven't decided yet."

"Getting a tattoo shouldn't be an impulsive decision," he said.

"Was yours?"

"No. Mine was well thought out."

Liam didn't want to talk about tattoos, especially his. But since Jane seemed interested in them and he wanted to keep things steady between them, he knew he would. He wrapped his arm around her waist and was glad when she didn't move away.

He led her down the hallway toward the food court and away from the tattoo parlor. He didn't try to make excuses for what he was doing. He wanted her away from there because he sensed she wasn't ready to make a decision about putting something permanent on her body. And he had an inkling that she'd do it just to prove to herself that she could.

"Where are we going?" she asked. She wore a pair of tight jeans and some sandals that left her toes bare. She had on a green, long-sleeved sweater that accented the color of her skin.

"I think I still owe you dessert," he said, grasping at straws to keep her from telling him to hit the road. He knew things were still a little too unsettled between them, and he was a guy who didn't always know the right thing to say.

"I don't eat after midnight," she said.

"That has good-girl rule written all over it."

"It has nothing to do with being good. For health reasons it's a bad idea to eat this late. Your metabolism slows down at night."

"I'm planning to get some exercise in later . . . you are, too, so I think you're safe." Time to find out how much damage had been done when he'd left her alone earlier.

"I'm not sure that you should count on that," she said.

"Count on what, having sex with you later?" he asked, just to tease her.

She flushed a little. "Yes."

"We're having a vacation fling, remember? We have to make the most of every moment." If there was an edge to his voice, he felt justified. He wanted her to say flat-out that he wasn't welcome in her bed anymore if that was the case.

"Well, I'm a little sore from earlier," she said.

Relief flooded him. She wasn't pushing him away. He wrapped his arm around her and drew her closer. "Then how do you feel about dancing?"

"How about we skip dessert and stop trying to find some activity to justify eating this late?"

"I've kind of had my heart set on sharing something special with you."

He led her down a covered walkway from the Royal Banner to the neighboring hotel where he knew the Krispy Kreme store was.

"Okay, but I want to hear the story behind your tattoo."

He stopped walking and drew her over to one of the benches under a window. "Why?"

"I'm not sure. But I can tell it's important to you and I want to know more about the man I slept with."

"Don't like having sex with a stranger?"

"Do you?"

"Not since I was too young and stupid to realize there is a difference between screwing around and making love."

She bit her lower lip. "So are you going to tell me about your four-leaf clover?"

"Hell. You know I made love to you, right?"

She lifted one shoulder in a delicate little shrug, the movement small and vulnerable. "I know you left as soon as you could."

"I came back," he said.

She didn't say anything else. He pulled her into his arms.

God, he hated—HATED—talking about his mom. And the tattoo was all about her.

"Yes, you did."

He had his arm wrapped around her shoulder and she tipped her head back, looking up at him. "I really like your tattoo. The colors aren't faded at all. Have you had it for long?"

"I got it when I was fourteen."

"Is that even legal?"

"Not really. As a kid I was tall for my age. When I was sixteen I could go to bars and not get carded."

"I know *that's* not legal."

"Um . . . I'm not the rule-follower you are."

"Didn't your dad care that you were doing those kinds of things?"

The old man had been busy at the firehouse. And busy trying to stay away from their home. As an adult, Liam still didn't understand the old man completely. But he suspected that coming home and not having their mom there was too much for the him. The house had seemed emptier without her laughter filling it.

"He worked a lot. Mostly it was up to my oldest brother Ian to ride herd on us."

"How much older?"

"Almost four years." He pulled his arm from behind Jane and leaned forward, resting his forearms on his thighs. "Anyway, by the time I was fourteen, Ian was a firefighter, too, and gone a lot. My brother Pat and I kind of ran wild for a few years."

"Is that when you got the tattoo?"

"Yes." There was no way he was going to tell Jane about the gang he and Pat had been running with or about the fact that they'd both almost died getting in a little over their heads. That night they'd both been shaken and made a pact with each other.

A few days later Liam had found himself in front of one of the dive tattoo parlors that used to line Main Street before it went all upscale. He'd gone inside and had a four-leaf clover put on his chest. Right over his heart so he'd always have his mom close by. Always have the protection of the O'Roarkes with him. And so he'd never forget that he wasn't alone in the world.

"Liam?"

"My mom liked them and I was thinking of her when I got it. It's my lucky charm."

Chapter 12

Jane excused herself to go to the bathroom while Liam went to buy donuts. She wasn't too sure where they were heading, but she felt much better now than she had earlier.

The hallway leading to the bathrooms wasn't crowded at all. Henry Banner exited the men's room as she approached. He wiped his hand over his face and stared at her for a moment, then smiled when he recognized her.

"What's up, Jane? Have you been back to the blackjack table?"

"No, I don't think gambling is in my blood. I tried craps and that was fun but so far I've resisted the urge to return to the casino and throw away my hard-earned money."

Henry grabbed her arm and pulled her to the side of the hallway. "Don't say that too loud or you might be kicked out of the hotel."

"I think I'm safe."

"Why? Chase is serious about the casino. It's the most important thing in his life."

Jane doubted that. Chase might be a workaholic but his job was demanding. His hotel never closed, and he was running a business that was being targeted by an arsonist.

"I think family is important to him as well," she said.

"I guess. But he will only give so much before he starts putting up rules."

She had no idea what he was talking about. "Are you okay, Henry?"

His breath didn't smell like the scotch she knew he liked to drink.

"Yeah, fine. Do you want to join me in the casino? Maybe your luck will rub off on me."

All this talk about luck made her realize the shimmering promise that was Las Vegas. She'd always been way too practical to ever let herself think that something as capricious as fate took any precedence in her life. But she had been counting on Vegas to change her life as well.

"I'm on a date."

"Too bad. Are you sure I can't talk you into ditching the guy?"

"Yes, I'm sure. Though he likes to gamble, so maybe we'll see you later."

She excused herself to go into the ladies' room. When she came out, Henry was gone and Liam was waiting at the end of the hallway.

"I've got the goods. Hot and fresh."

He was really obsessed with those donuts, she thought. She searched the food court to see if Henry was still hanging out. She was a little concerned after his rambling conversation and awkward behavior. "I'm just not a donut person."

"You haven't experienced it the right way," he said. "What are you looking for?"

"Henry Banner. Did you see him?"

"No, where was he?"

"In the hallway there. He was acting weird."

"Weird how?"

"Just saying things that made no sense. But he hadn't been drinking . . . at least, not as far as I could tell."

"I hope he's not using again."

Jane had no idea that Chase and Liam were that tight, or that Chase would discuss the problems in the Banner family.

"How do you know about Henry's problems?"

"Chase and I have been friends for over twenty years."

"Close friends, then?" she asked. Shanna was her oldest friend—she'd never really been the type to keep in touch with people once they moved away or changed jobs.

"Yes," he said, sitting down at one of the café-style tables in the food court. He was so tall and big that he looked uncomfortable as he sat down in the chair.

"Normally I wouldn't have brought a date along with him and Wendy."

"Then why did you tonight?" she asked, trying to understand the curveball he'd just thrown her. She sat across from him. The hubbub of people going in and out of the area was loud but not as intrusive as it would have been with anyone else. Probably because Liam focused on her, making her feel like she was the only person in the place.

"I wanted to spend time with you and I'd already made plans with them."

Which told her exactly nothing, something she was sure he knew.

"What did you mean by Henry *using*? Using what? He didn't smell like pot or anything like that."

"Meth."

"Meth? What are the symptoms? His eyes weren't dilated."

"Damn, this is exactly what Chase doesn't need right now."

Jane agreed. "Should we call him? I mean, Henry's an adult so whatever he does . . ."

"You're right."

Jane slipped her hand into Liam's. "How bad is the problem?"

"Bad enough for Henry to have been disinherited a few years ago."

Jane's own family was too close-knit to do anything like that, but then again they didn't have a multimillion-dollar business, either. "He doesn't seem too bitter about it."

"If he stays clean, then Chase will give him an opportunity to buy back into the business."

"Has he?"

"I don't know. From what you said, maybe not."

"It might have been nothing," she said, not wanting to cause any trouble for the Banners. She liked Henry.

"Well, that's Chase's problem, not ours. Are you ready to try the best yeast donut in the world?"

"You're crazy, you know that?"

"You're not the first to mention it."

Liam didn't want his night with Jane to end, but she was clearly fading as they walked out of the European-style revue. The show was fun and not something he usually took in while he was in Vegas, but Jane had suggested it.

She'd been shocked when the dancers had come out in their costumes with only pasties covering their nipples. But by the end of the show she'd gotten past it.

"Those costumes look really heavy—I wonder how much time those girls have to spend in the gym."

That wasn't something he'd given a lot of thought to. "I have no idea."

"I bet they go at least a couple of hours every day. I couldn't achieve that type of muscle definition without a lot of time at the gym."

He liked the thought of Jane in one those costumes. "Want me to ask Chase if he'll loan you one of those outfits?"

"No—didn't you hear what I said? I need more time at the gym before I can pull that off."

"Just a private show," he said, keeping her tucked close to his side as they moved through the crowd.

"Have you been to one of these shows before?" she asked.

"Yes, a few times. I brought my brother Rory out here last year for his birthday—he's an investment banker. That's a new thing for him, so I didn't expect him to have issues with gambling."

He was still coming to terms with the changes in his little brother, but Liam had to admit Rory seemed happier now than he ever had when he was a firefighter.

"Why did he?"

"He didn't like the 'risk-to-pay-off odds'."

"Sounds like a smart man."

Liam shrugged. Rory was whip-smart but he was always street-smart too, which Liam knew counted more than book learning. At least in his experience.

"I've never seen a show like that before. One time some girls from the office wanted to go to a strip club after work but I couldn't get up the nerve to go."

"Why not?"

"I can barely look at myself naked, much less someone else."

"You didn't seem to have any problems looking at my body," Liam said.

"You're different."

"How?"

She shrugged. "I can't explain it."

He thought about teasing her until she gave him an answer but he knew she was stubborn enough to keep her silence when it mattered. So why wasn't he sharing the fact that he was in Vegas to investigate arson? He knew she was trustworthy.

But he didn't want to start depending on her, only to

have her walk out the door on him. And they'd agreed to a short-term affair so that was exactly what she'd do.

He knew that he deliberately kept his affairs brief so that he couldn't ever start depending on a woman. He'd talked to a therapist about it once. The session was supposed to be about the three kids he'd found huddled in a closet dead from smoke inhalation but instead he'd gotten caught up in his own abandonment issues. The way his mom's death had left a big, aching emptiness.

Fuck, why was this surfacing now? He glanced down at Jane as they walked through the crowd. What was it about her that made him wish . . . ah, hell, he was getting over this as quick as possible.

"I've noticed that all the casinos have shows billed as European . . . that means topless but tasteful, right?"

"Yeah," he said, trying to keep up with the conversation when what he really wanted to do was toss her over his shoulder—fireman's carry style—and take her away. He didn't want to talk about other scantily clad women. He wanted to see her bare body.

He needed to stake his claim on her and ensure that she wasn't going anywhere until he was good and ready to let her. But life didn't come with guarantees. Hell, he knew that and usually he was live and let live.

"Liam?"

"What?"

"I asked if you'd ever been to a strip club," she said. "Are you okay?"

"Yes, I've been to a strip club. Pat's girlfriend dances at one."

"Your brother?"

"Yeah, don't you want to know about their exercise routines?"

She pulled away from him. "Are you being facetious?"

No, he was trying to pick a fight. It had been too long since he'd gotten into it with anyone. And he'd much rather argue with Jane than keep going to the place he was in his head.

"What's going on? If my questions are out of line, I'm sorry."

He shook his head. "I'm the one who's sorry. I keep thinking about my mom."

Her eyes widened. "Was your mom a stripper?"

"No. And the correct term is *exotic dancer*."

"What made you think of her?"

Probably all those questions she'd been asking earlier about his tattoo. He shrugged. "She's just on my mind."

Jane didn't say anything else but wrapped her arm around his waist and leaned against him as they walked back to the lobby of the hotel. He knew he'd revealed way more than he'd wanted to with the comments he'd made. But he couldn't regret it. There was something about Jane that made him almost want to expose his deepest secrets.

At the elevator bank he hesitated, not wanting to force her into spending the night with him, but she kept her arm around him. "Will you come up with me? I want to spend the night in your arms."

He couldn't resist that invitation and didn't even try. "Yes."

He knew that this was part of the illusion of Vegas, but a sense of rightness settled deep inside him as they entered her room.

Liam didn't expect to sleep so soundly through the night but he had. Jane was like a new addiction and he loved the feel of her pressed up against him. Wearing only her cream-colored negligee, she'd fallen asleep in his arms.

Sunlight spilled through the gap where the drapes didn't

quite meet. He glanced at his watch. He was supposed to meet with Didi this morning, and he wanted time to call Chase and find out if Henry was using again.

If Henry was, then he was going on the suspects list . . . straight to the top.

He pushed himself out of bed because he wanted to linger. He wanted to pull her into his arms and hold her tightly so he knew she'd be right by his side.

"Liam?"

"Right here," he said, sinking back down next to her. If he wasn't careful, he'd lose his focus completely.

"Is it morning already?" she asked, leaning up to kiss his thigh just below his boxer briefs. He'd thought sleeping partially clothed would make it easier to keep his hands to himself. But it hadn't. He'd stroked and kissed her last night, bringing her to an orgasm during the middle of the night.

"Lie down with me," she said, pulling the covers back and beckoning him into the nest of blankets.

He lay down beside her. She wrapped herself around him, his morning hard-on pressing against her hip.

"Yes." He took her mouth in his, letting his hands wander over her body.

Her stomach growled and he laughed. "Hungry?"

She buried her red face against his chest. "Yes."

"You should have had a donut last night," he said.

"Stop it. You're like a donut pusher."

He laughed and got out of the bed. He opened up the minibar. "Peanuts, candy bars, or chips?"

"Peanuts."

"Salted or honey-roasted?"

"Honey-roasted."

He popped open the can as he crossed back to the bed, pouring some into her hand. She ate half of the can. "I'm full now."

"Good. Where were we?" he asked.

"You were under the covers with me."

"You were going to take off your nightgown first."

"I was?"

"Yes."

She shifted around and then pulled it off, tossing it on the floor at his feet. He pushed the covers to the foot of the bed. "You look better than any of the women we saw in the show last night."

She was rosy and flushed but she didn't cover herself up. He trailed his finger over her breasts. She shivered with awareness and her nipples tightened. He traced a random pattern around each of her breasts, coming close to her nipples but not caressing the beaded flesh.

He leaned down to lick each nipple until it tightened. Then he blew gently on the tips. She raked her nails down his back.

He shifted on the bed, stretching out next to her, propping himself up on his elbow so he could watch her while he ran his hand down her body.

He drew her nipples out by suckling them, then nibbled his way down her body. "Have you ever thought of piercing your navel?"

"No," she said, her voice breathless.

"A charm right here would be very sexy," he said, running his tongue over her belly button.

He shifted up over her, kneeling between her thighs and staring down at the neat curls that covered her femininity. She swallowed, her hands shifting on the bed next to her hips.

"Open yourself for me," he said.

"Liam . . ."

"Come on, baby, show me you want me."

Her legs moved but he took her hands in his, bringing them to her mound. She hesitated, but then she pulled those lower lips apart. The pink of her flesh looked so delicate and soft—tempting. He couldn't wait to taste her.

"Hold still," he said.

He leaned down, blowing lightly on her before tonguing that soft flesh. She lifted her hips toward his mouth.

He drew her flesh into his mouth, sucking carefully on her. He drew his hands up her thighs, bending them back toward her body until she was completely open to him. He pushed his finger into her body and drew out some of her moisture, then lifted his head and looked up at her.

Her eyes were closed, her head tipped back and her shoulders arched, throwing her breasts forward with their berry-hard tips, begging for more attention.

He lowered his head again, hungry for more of her. He feasted on her body the way a starving man would, eating out the moist flesh between her legs. He used his teeth, tongue, and fingers to bring her to the brink of climax but held her there, wanting to draw out the moment of completion until she was begging him for it.

Her hands grasped his head as she thrust her hips up toward his face, but he pulled back so she didn't get the contact she craved.

"Liam, please."

He scraped his teeth over her clitoris and she screamed as her orgasm rocked through her body. He kept his mouth on her until her body stopped shuddering and then slid up beside her.

"Your turn," she said, pushing him over onto his back. She pushed his boxer briefs down his legs and he kicked free of them.

She took his erection in her hand and he felt a drop of pre-cum at the head. She leaned down to lick it off, then stroked his penis with a firm grip that made him gasp.

She followed her hand with her tongue, teasing him with quick licks and light touches. She massaged his sac and then pressed lower. She squeezed his balls and then made a ring with her thumb and forefinger around the base of his shaft. Her mouth encircled the tip of him and she began to suck.

He arched on the bed, thrusting up into her before he realized what he was doing. He pulled her from his body, wanting to be inside her when he came, not in her mouth.

He pulled her up his body until she straddled his hips. The feel of their naked loins pressed together made him realize he needed a condom. He fumbled around for his pants, which he'd left on the floor by the bed. He took out the condom and put it on. Then, using his grip on her hips, he pulled her down while he pushed his erection into her body.

He thrust harder and harder, trying to get deeper. He pulled her legs forward, forcing them farther apart until she settled even closer to him.

He slid deeper still into her. She arched her back, reaching up to entwine her arms around his shoulders. He thrust harder and felt every nerve in his body tensing. Reaching between their bodies, he touched her between her legs until he felt her body start to tighten around him.

He came in a rush, continuing to thrust into her until his body was drained. He then collapsed on top of her, laying his head between her breasts. She rested right over his tattoo—he felt the soft kiss she dropped there and closed his eyes, letting the emotions he felt for her swamp him for this moment.

Chapter 13

Jane woke for the second time to find the room quiet and empty. A note from Liam was on the pillow right next to her head. It was the first thing she saw when she opened her eyes. She picked it up.

If you can do lunch, call me. If not, text me your schedule. Liam.

Wow, she thought. What an unromantic note. She rubbed a hand over her eyes. Not everyone had the soul of a poet. She found her BlackBerry on the table and scrolled through her e-mails.

Nothing pressing or urgent. She sat down on the bed—it smelled of Liam and sex. She closed her eyes and felt a wave of despair wash over her. What the hell was she doing?

She needed to talk to someone but had no idea what she'd say. Shanna would give her a high-five and tell her that it was about time she started really living. Her mom would . . . her mom would have that worried tone in her voice that she always seemed to have lately. She didn't understand the changes Jane had made in her clothes and her hair and hadn't exactly approved of Jane going to Vegas on vacation.

Her phone rang a few minutes later. The guest room phone, not her cell. She rolled over to answer it.

"Hello?"

"Hello, Jane."

Liam.

"Did you get my note?"

"Uh, yes."

"It was too short, right? I was worried about that."

She wondered where he was but didn't want to ask. She remembered a television show that her studio produced about people living in Vegas, and the tag line had been *only take risks you're willing to pay for.*

She thought sleeping with Liam had been a risk. Not because of any health reason but because of this emotion. She rolled over and hugged his pillow to her chest.

"It wasn't too short. I haven't checked my schedule for the day yet so I don't know if I'm free for lunch."

"Let me know when you can. Do you have time to do me a favor?"

"What kind of favor?"

There was silence in the background and she thought he must have gone back to his room. The casino would be louder, with the unmistakable ringing bells.

"Will you ask Wendy to go shopping with you and try to find out if Henry is using again?"

Why didn't Liam take care of this himself? She was essentially a stranger to the Banner family. Definitely not someone Wendy would talk to.

"Why don't you just ask Chase?"

"I can't—he had to fly to Monaco to handle something at his casino there."

She tucked her hair behind her ear. "Okay, I'll call her when we get off the phone."

"Thanks, Jane. You have my cell number now, so call me as soon as you know your schedule."

"Where are you?" she asked. She couldn't stand not knowing one more second.

"In my bungalow, but I'm going to talk while I head up to the lobby. I wish I could have stayed in bed with you all day but I'd already made these plans."

She understood that but a part of her yearned to have him still with her. He'd come to Vegas to gamble and she knew that she'd never be able to come between him and the poker room.

"Are you going to be playing poker later? I can stop by the casino."

"Don't do that. I think Jameson is hoping to coax you into being his lady fortune."

"You don't need me for that," she said, thinking of his tattoo. "Do you?"

"No, I don't. But I do need you for something else."

"What?"

"For you, Jane. I need you for you. Because you're making my life richer by just being in it."

She caught her breath. "Did you read that on a greeting card?"

He laughed. "Don't you think I can make up something like that?"

"No. If you were that kind of guy, then I wouldn't have gotten such a brusque note."

She heard the sounds of people talking in the background. "I knew that note wasn't right, but I didn't have time to rethink it."

"Really, it's okay."

"Did you find the pastry bag yet?"

"Uh, no. Where is it?"

"On the table by the window."

She glanced over and saw the unmistakable green-and-white donut bag. "How'd you get them in my room?"

"I have my ways. Don't forget—you're going to call Wendy."

"I won't. You don't have to remind me."

"Sorry about that. Old habit."

"You're late," she heard a woman say in the background.

"Liam?"

"I've got to run. Talk to you later, baby."

"'Bye, Liam."

She wanted to linger on the line and hope to hear that woman's voice again. But she didn't. Instead she hung up and tried to remind herself that she trusted Liam.

Did she really? This was probably why she never had had a temporary affair before, she realized. This sinking feeling in her stomach that couldn't be fixed by eating.

She just wasn't cut out for temporary. Memories of the night before flooded her and she remembered how closely he held her after they'd made love the last time. It had felt like more than it should have.

She reminded herself that he hadn't made any promises and she wasn't looking for them. Honestly, she wasn't. But the vow sounded hollow, even in her mind.

"You're late," Didi said as he approached her in the lobby. She wore a skirt that hit her knee and a pair of leather boots that cupped her calves. She had on a black turtle neck sweater, and for Didi she looked almost conservative.

"Only five minutes."

She gave him a disgusted look. "Five minutes is going to make a difference as far as traffic is concerned."

"I'm sorry."

Didi brushed past him and out the door. Her car was parked in the driveway and Liam tipped the bellman who had been watching it. Didi got behind the wheel.

"What's up?"

"I just don't like being late."

He gave her a wry glance. "You always build an extra ten minutes into our schedule."

"Well, now there's only five," she snapped.

He reached over to stop her from putting the car in gear. "Seriously, Didi, what's wrong?"

She shook her head, her long blond hair brushing over her shoulders. "I saw my ex last night."

He didn't do relationship conversations. "Where?"

"At the fire."

He must have been one of the guest-witnesses that she went to interview. "Ah, hell, you should have said something. I would have questioned them."

"He wasn't a witness."

"You dated a guy on the LVFD?" he asked. "Is that why you have the no firefighter's rule when it comes to dating?"

"No. He's an ATF officer. He was called in to investigate the Banner Casino fires."

"Who is he?"

"Tod Courtney."

Liam had heard of the guy but never met him. "I think Chase spoke to him after the first fire."

"That's what our notes indicate."

"Are you going to be prickly all morning? You're ruining my good mood."

"I haven't had any coffee yet," she said. The miles rolled by.

"Why are you in a good mood?"

"Just feeling lucky today." He wasn't going to talk about Jane. He didn't even have anything figured out for himself yet but he knew she made him feel better. Made the investigation and the frustration he felt at not having a solid lead kind of dissipate.

"Glad someone is. Did you do anything to narrow down our list of suspects?"

"As a matter of fact, I think we need to add one more," he said. He'd never seriously considered Henry a suspect before this because the guy just seemed not to care about anything other than drinking, gambling, and having fun. And Henry just didn't seem smart enough to pull off the fires.

"Who?"

"Henry Banner." If Henry was using again, then he had to be on the list because he was a different person when the drug had control of him. Violent and angry. Liam had seen Henry break the furniture in Chase's office while on one of his highs.

"Hate to break it to you but he's already on my list," Didi said.

"I'm going to go over the notes on the first fire."

"Why?"

"Because if Henry's our man, I'm guessing the first one was an accident."

"What's the motive?" Didi asked. "Financial?"

"No, he no longer holds stock in the company."

"That's interesting. Why didn't Chase mention this when he gave us his list of suspects?"

"He probably doesn't think his brother is our fire-starter."

"Do you?" Didi asked.

"I'm not sure. I want to take a look at everything we have."

"Would Henry know enough about the security system to bypass it?"

"That's the million-dollar question," Liam said. The sun was bright this morning and the air was crisp and cool, especially considering he was a Florida boy. But the air felt good against his skin. "Then move him to the top. I ran into him last night and he was acting weird."

"Weird how?"

What had Jane said? "Talking in long, rambling sentences and jumping from subject to subject. In light of the fire last night . . ."

Didi made a left turn, changing lanes. "I'll track him down when we're done with this meeting and see what I can find out. Did you know that Chase left Las Vegas this morning?"

"Yes, he sent me a message."

"Do you think he's running?" Didi asked.

Liam hoped like hell not. Because he still trusted Chase, and their friendship had lasted more than twenty years. He and Chase weren't drinking buddies—they were friends.

"My gut says no. He does have a legitimate reason to be in Europe right now, and his wife and kids are still here."

"Not all men are rock-solid; some of them do leave their wives holding the bag. Did you get to confirm if one of the kids was really sick last night?"

That sounded way too personal for Liam to comment on, so he let it go. Didi was letting more slip this morning than she usually did. Liam wondered if it was this case and their lack of solid leads or if it was the mysterious Todd Courtney fire marshal who had her so rattled.

"No." Liam didn't have Jane's cell phone number or he could text her to ask about the kids when she saw Wendy later. Instead he'd have to call the Banner house and see what was going on there. "I'll find out this morning. Take a drive out to their place and see if everything's normal."

"Good."

She pulled into the parking lot and turned off the car but made no move to get out.

There was little work that needed her attention, so Jane had no excuse not to call Wendy Banner and see if she wanted to go shopping. Except she really didn't want to spend the day walking around some mall.

But Liam had asked her to and she'd given her word. Her promises, and her willingness to deliver on them, were something she liked about herself. She dialed the number Wendy had given her the night before and made plans to meet her at the Las Vegas Fashion Show Mall.

"Ready for a little retail therapy?" Wendy asked as she joined Jane at the Starbucks on the lower level.

"Of course—it's my favorite kind of therapy. How are the kids? Which one was sick?"

"Gracie—she had a fever but we got it under control overnight. Chase had to leave for a business trip so I'm glad her fever came down. He won't leave if one of the kids is sick."

"That's nice," Jane said as they started walking down the promenade.

"Yes, it is. As much as I resent all the time he spends at the casinos, he really does step up when I need him to."

"Is family that important?"

"Isn't it to everyone?"

"I guess. My brother is more concerned with his globe-trotting," she said, hoping that Wendy would take the hint and talk about Henry.

"Oh, siblings are different from family. You aren't married, right?"

"Divorced."

"So you kind of know how it is when you become a couple and start a new life."

She wished. Rodney had never really been interested in doing anything as a couple that set them apart from her family. An orphan who'd never cared to find out who his biological parents were, Rodney had never been adopted and spent most of his formative years in a group home. When they'd gotten married, Jane had tried to let her family be his. "My family is kind of overwhelming. During my marriage we did everything with my parents."

Wendy stopped walking. "Well, maybe that's why you're divorced."

Jane had told no one the circumstances of her divorce, not her parents or Shanna. She just nodded in vague agreement. Wendy had the kind of confidence that Jane had never been able to find outside of her career. Jane never would have guessed that she could be happy as a stay-at-home mom, but she suspected if she had been more like Wendy she might have been.

"I'm sorry—that was completely out of line. Chase is always telling me to watch what I say when I'm entertaining the wives and girlfriends of the big rollers."

"Do you have to do that a lot?" Jane asked. Somehow she'd figure out a way to bring Henry up.

"More than I like to. Some of them aren't too bad."

They went into the Louis Vuitton store and Jane found herself buying a purse and wallet even though she didn't need them.

Wendy was a power shopper and Jane had a little trouble keeping up with her. As they approached Abercrombie & Fitch she noticed the shirtless model posed at the entrance— really, how could she miss a guy with a chest like that?

"He looks a little like your brother-in-law, Henry."

Wendy gave a little laugh. "Very little. Henry hasn't ever seen the inside of a gym. How do you know him?"

"We met at the blackjack table."

"That sounds about right. He spends all of his time in the casinos."

"Working like Chase?" Jane asked.

"No, nothing like Chase. Henry has . . . he has his own problems."

"Oh, what kind of problems? I asked him if he was addicted to gambling but he just laughed and said taking risks was in his blood."

"That's true. When I first met Chase the Royal Banner

wasn't as prestigious as it is today. The family had properties all over the world but they all looked like they had in
the 70s, and newer casinos were taking over the Strip.

"But Chase worked hard to turn that around. It was
touch-and-go there for a while."

"Not now?"

"No. I mean, the fires aren't exactly helping the bottom
line but the company is really solid now."

"Is that how come Henry can spend so much time gambling?"

Wendy shrugged. "Who knows why he does what he
does?"

Jane realized Wendy wasn't going to talk about Henry with
her. And she couldn't blame the other woman, but Henry's
behavior last night really concerned her. She stopped walking.

"I'm sorry if this is out of line, but last night when I saw
Henry he was acting really weird. Liam mentioned that
Henry used to have a drug problem and I guess I'm . . . con-
cerned."

Wendy switched her packages from one hand to the other.
"Damn, I really hope you're wrong. Chase doesn't need this
right now."

"I do, too. I don't know him very well, so I could be."

"But you wouldn't have brought it up if you didn't think
there was a possibility that he did have a problem," Wendy
said.

"Yes."

"Is that the only reason you asked me to go shopping?"

"Uh, no. I needed to get away from the hotel for a
while."

"And away from Liam?"

Jane shrugged. "I guess it's nice just to have some time to
myself where I don't have to think about anything."

Wendy laughed again, her smile one of understanding. "Retail therapy, Jane. It's the only thing that keeps me sane."

Jane wasn't too sure if it would keep her sane, but it did take her mind off of Liam and reinforce the idea that this wasn't her real life. Vacation shopping, vacation fling—they should both be things that made her feel good.

Chapter 14

Liam leaned forward, bracing his arms on the conference table. Tod Courtney had done a detailed report of everything they knew so far. Tucker Fields from Hot Heads, Inc. was going to be conferenced into the meeting and had sent a PowerPoint deck that Liam took down the hall to make copies of.

"Do you need help with that?" Didi asked.

"No, I think I got it," Liam said. "Why didn't you stay in the conference room?"

"Tod was there," she said. "I didn't want to start discussing the case without you."

He refrained from pointing out that she could have caught him up on anything that she and Tod discussed. "What's up with you two?"

She shrugged. "Nothing much. I know it seems like I'm off my game but I'm still adjusting to seeing him. He usually works on the East Coast."

"So do we," Liam said, taking the copies from the machine and leading the way back to the conference room. He glanced at Didi's pale face and knew he needed to do something to get her mind off of Tod and her personal relationship with the man.

"He's a forensic accountant." Liam interjected a note of sarcasm into his voice.

"Yeah, what of it?"

"*Accountant*, Didi."

"Shut up."

She pushed past him and entered the conference room with all her usual confidence. Tod stood at the front of the room. The fire marshal was there as well as two firemen who'd been the first on the scene at fire number one. They would be breaking down all four fires this morning and talking individually to everyone involved.

Tod got the meeting started as soon as Tucker was on the speaker phone. "Thanks for coming to the meeting today. I want to determine if the fires at the Banner Casinos is arson-for-profit. I know that Didi and Liam have found concrete evidence for arson, so we just want to go forward from this point."

"The team from Hot Heads have been researching a financial motive for the fires . . . Tucker, what have you found?"

The ATF was involved because the fires had caused over a million dollars in damage.

"There's not a clear-cut financial motive that we can find in the account of the hotel itself. The fire damage has actually caused the profit to drop, and even though he's insured with full replacement value on the casinos, Banner makes more money staying open and keeping the people at his poker tables."

"Can we rule him out as a suspect?" Liam asked.

"I'm leaning that way. We're waiting for one other report to come back. There's a pattern of fire history."

"What pattern?" Didi asked.

"About fifteen years ago there was a fire at the Royal Banner in Atlantic City. I don't have the report yet—it's in an archive. Hard to remember that fifteen years ago we were still hand-writing everything."

Tod made a few notes on his papers and Liam noted that

the man seemed really thorough and a bit of a stick-in-the-mud. What did Didi see in the guy?

"Did Banner Casinos increase their insurance coverage recently?" Tod asked.

"Yes, but that seems tied to the renovated wing," Didi said.

Liam flipped through his packet and found the information to back up Didi's statement. "Page four of the insurance rider."

Everyone flipped to the page, and Liam leaned back in his chair to get more comfortable. His cell phone vibrated in his pocket and he pulled it out, glancing at the caller ID. It was a text message from Tucker.

T.Fields@hotheads.com: I'm sending you a file with all the information we discussed. When the meeting ends call me.

L.ORoarke@hotheads.com: I will. I need you to look at Henry Banner as a suspect.

T.Fields@hotheads.com: What's up?

L.ORoarke@hotheads.com: Heavy drug user in the past might be trying to work some financial angle on his own.

"Liam?"

He looked up at Tod—apparently he'd missed something. "I'm sorry, what?"

"Do you have anything else to add?"

He gave Didi a quick glance. "On Chase. I told Tod he'd left for Europe this morning."

"Other than the fact that he said he'd be in touch as soon as he landed."

"Does anyone else stand to profit from the hotel personally if it goes up in flames?" Tod asked.

Liam flipped through the pages. "Just the Banner Casino Group."

162 / Katherine Garbera

"So that rules out finances. Because of the damage amounts, someone from our office will still be involved. We want to ensure an arrest."

"I think we all do," Didi said.

"Definitely. Tod, can you do some financial investigating on Henry Banner?"

"He's not listed as a principle investor in the company," Tod said.

"I know, but he and Chase have had some problems in the past and money might be motivating him now."

"I'll look into it," Tod said.

"Didi has all the information if you need to talk to someone."

"Great. We can discuss it over lunch." Tod smiled over at Didi and she gave him one of her icy stares.

"I'm working the revenge angle and have an interview this afternoon with one of the Banners' main competitors, who was driven out of business by them."

"Bradley Jameson?"

"Yes."

They all discussed the next steps as the meeting broke up. Liam went outside to call Tucker back but noticed he'd missed a call from Jane.

Jane left a voice mail for Liam when she got back to the hotel, letting him know that she wouldn't be available until later in the day. In her old rule-abiding days she'd have sat in her room waiting for him to call her back. But no more.

She wasn't needed at her job but she wanted—no, needed— to have a break from Liam for the afternoon. She changed into her bikini and went down to the pool area to meet up with Shanna.

Her friend was lounging near the bar, where music blared from the speakers. The pool was crowded and there weren't any vacant chairs but Shanna had saved her one.

"How'd the date go last night?" Shanna asked as soon as Jane sat down next to her.

Blue October's "Hate Me" blared from the speakers and Jane tried to tune it out. The song never failed to make her realize how much she did hate herself. She didn't have the kind of sick thoughts or anger that the lead singer did, but she did have stuff about herself that she wished she could change.

Still. Dang it. She didn't know why she'd expected one trip to make such a drastic difference in her life. Or one night with Liam. But today she still felt like old Jane.

"Jane? You still with me, girl?"

"Yeah. The date was good," she said at last, thinking that evening had been beyond anything she'd experienced before. All in all, it was the best date of her life and she was struggling to remember that Liam was a temporary lover.

"Just good? I gave you fabulous hair and makeup, Janie."

"Fabulous, then. Thanks for doing that, by the way. I'm going to try to recreate that look tonight."

"I don't mind helping you out again," Shanna said.

"I mind. I like to do things for myself."

"Well, product is the key to doing it."

Jane shook her head at her friend. "We sound like a couple of boring old ladies."

"Speak for yourself. Hair care is a young issue. Look at all those heiresses on the covers of magazines and all over the Internet—you can't tell me they aren't concerned about hair care."

She had to laugh at the way Shanna said it. "But you do have a point. We should do something exciting."

"Like what?" Jane asked tentatively.

"Bungee jumping," Shanna said. "I've already been once this week and I want to go back."

"No way," Jane said. Sure, she wanted to change, but *dead*

wasn't exactly the change she was searching for. Besides, extreme stuff like this was more Marcus's type of thing.

"Give me one good reason not to," Shanna said.

"Ah, you have to jump off a bridge or building to do it." This was a crazy idea, but it was different and she felt a restlessness that she'd never experienced before. She wanted to experience as much of Vegas as she could.

"Are you afraid of heights?" Shanna asked.

"Not when I'm in a building looking out a window, but dying or severely injuring myself isn't exactly what I had planned for today."

Shanna pulled her sunglasses down to the edge of her nose and looked at Jane. "That's old Jane talking."

She liked old Jane, especially if that meant she didn't have to try something like bungee jumping. "Convince me to give it a try."

"I've done it twice before. It's exhilarating and it makes you feel like . . . like you can survive anything. Actually, the more I think about it, the more convinced I am that this is the perfect thing for you to try."

"I don't know about this," she said, unable to believe she was actually contemplating doing it. Jane's stomach tightened at the thought of trying a bungee jump, but she'd also felt a little queasy when she'd had to talk to Liam last night about being only her second lover.

She looked deep into her soul, searched for the conviction to do this. To make another real change in her life, another giant step away from the woman she was to the woman she was becoming.

"Is it close by?"

"Yes, right next to Circus Circus. They have a big T-tower. It's owned by AJ Hackett. They have a bunch of pictures and stuff on him at the place. He's a living legend in the world of bungee jumping."

Jane almost said yes but then she realized that bungee

jumping wasn't really a change she wanted to make. If she did it, it would only be to prove to Shanna that she wasn't a coward, and at the end of the day that wasn't what this year was supposed to be about.

"I'll walk over with you and watch you jump."

"Are you sure you don't want to try it?"

"Maybe I'll change my mind once we get over there," Jane said, but she wasn't too sure of that. She'd have to do a lot of research on the sport before she even considered jumping. And then she'd call Marcus and ask him to come jump with her. Except her brother would probably tease her to death.

"Jane?"

"Yeah?"

"Want to head over there now?"

Jane nodded. If nothing else, her time in Vegas was exposing her to many different sides of life. And things she'd never contemplated when she was at home in L.A. But then, Vegas was all about risk.

Liam finished up at the fire marshal's office later than he'd expected. He took his time getting back to the hotel. After the message from Jane, he figured she was trying to give them both some breathing room. The problem was, he didn't want any breathing room.

He wanted to find her and bind her to his side. Find a way to keep her there. But instead he had to have a talk with Jameson. Tucker had discovered some information that indicated that Jameson Bradley was a partial partner in the C&H hotel, which meant that he stood to gain if the hotel burnt down.

But the fires set at each of the properties felt more like revenge fires to Liam. The blazes hadn't gotten big enough fast enough to destroy the entire property. Everyone who was involved in investigating the fires agreed on that. They weren't going to rule anything out yet which chafed Liam a little.

Slow and steady was definitely the way of all arson investigations, but it wasn't his way. He wanted to see results, not just a tentative name crossed off a list.

Jameson was on a twenty-minute break, according to Matthew, who was his VIP host. The resorts assigned a host or hostess to their high rollers. Matthew's role was basically to keep Jameson happy so he'd stay at the Royal Banner and gamble instead of going to another resort. Which made it easier for Liam to find the man.

Jameson was in a strip club called Club Paradise. Liam took a cab to the club, located across the street from the Hard Rock Hotel.

He was ushered inside to one of the VIP rooms, where Jameson was enjoying a lap dance from a woman beautiful enough to grace the cover of *Vogue* magazine. Her body was fit and trim, her breasts large but not overblown or out of proportion to her body.

"O'Roarke, come on in and join us."

Liam stepped inside and took a seat. The girls working in Club Paradise were very beautiful and dressed in sexy formal wear. Liam had been here once before with Chase. The club had been around for a while, and women were actually welcome here. The sophisticated atmosphere of the club seemed to put them more at ease.

When the girl with Jameson finished her dance, he tipped her and then told her to come back later. "What's doing? Haven't seen much of you this trip."

"I'm not feeling the tables the way I usually am—I'm taking a break from gambling."

"Does that have anything to with the lady I saw you with the other night?"

Did it? Jane would be a convenient excuse, especially since he was going to ask Jameson some pointed questions about his business dealings with Chase. But he didn't want to talk about her with a man like Jameson.

"Maybe. Or maybe it's just all the funky shit happening at the hotel."

"The fires?"

"Yeah. Makes it hard for a man to concentrate on gambling."

"I hear you. I was ready to check out and move over to the Venetian, but Matthew was able to put together a sweet offer that convinced me to stay at the Royal."

"Good for you. Do you ever miss the old days when you were an owner?"

"Not really. There was too much pressure, you know, always watching the bottom line and trying to keep the business going."

As Jameson offered Liam a cigar, one of the girls came over to light them. The VIP room had a private cocktail waitress and they both ordered drinks.

"I'll tell you one thing I miss about being an owner."

"What's that?" Liam asked.

"The privileges that clubs like this one offer. Chase doesn't take as much advantage of them. Damn, his wife keeps him on a short chain, doesn't she?"

Chase didn't mind it. Liam knew that there were two places Chase liked to be at his resorts: working and keeping his players happy, and at home with his family. "All the trouble he's having is what's keeping him on a short leash."

"That's true. It's starting to seem like someone has a hard-on for the Banners, doesn't it?"

"Yeah, it does. You know anyone who doesn't like them enough to start fires in their properties?"

"Hell, every other casino on the Strip. The small ones fighting to compete with his hotel, and the ones owned by big corporations."

"But no one specifically gunning for Chase?"

"I don't think so. Why do you care?" Jameson asked, leaning over to put his cigar on the edge of the ashtray.

"Chase is a friend of mine."

"And you like a good fight," Jameson said with a grin.

"I'm not looking for anyone's ass to kick. Just trying to see if I can get a line on something that Chase can use to figure this out."

Jameson leaned back in the chair and signaled one of the girls to come over again. "I paid for three lap dances, O'Roarke. You're welcome to one."

The only one that Liam wanted to dance on his lap was Jane. And he was secure enough in his masculinity that he could decline and not worry about what Jameson thought. "Thanks, but not today."

"That brunette, right?"

"Leave it alone."

"Hey, I answered all of *your* questions."

"True, but I don't recall that I said anything about it being a trade."

Liam still didn't have the answers he was looking for as far as the fires were concerned. Jameson had just confirmed his every suspicion. And he'd done a little to clear himself from being a suspect. But he had the feeling that Jameson wouldn't lose any sleep if Chase was driven out of business by the arsonist. In fact, few people on the Strip would. After all, another corporation would just take over the land and keep the poker tables open.

Chapter 15

Jane stood outside the AJ Hackett bungee jumping center waiting for Shanna. They'd run into Mitchell and two other people from the studio in the lobby of the hotel and they'd decided to make a party of the bungee jump. Jane went along but felt so clearly out of her element that it was all she could do to keep a fake smile on her face.

She needed a break from the pressure that everyone was placing on her, trying to talk her into going on the bungee jump, so she was sitting outside waiting for the shuttle van from the hotel. She was in the portico going into the hotel when she heard someone call her name.

She glanced back to see Liam getting out of a cab. He wore a pair of faded jeans and a dark blue dress shirt. He'd left the collar open, making the shirt seem more casual.

"Do you have time for dinner?" he asked.

She glanced at her Rolex and saw that it was a little after six. She didn't know how to act around him. Was it all going to be casual between them now? She wanted to reach out and brush his hair back from his forehead where the wind had blown some of the strands but she wasn't sure she had the right to.

"I'd like to have dinner with you. Do you think we'll be able to get in at this hour?"

"I have some connections—we shouldn't have any problems. What have you been up to this afternoon?" he asked.

"Well, I was at that AJ Hackett place."

"The bungee jump center?"

"Is there really more than one place named after him?"

He pulled her close and kissed her quick. "Very funny. Did you jump?"

"Ah, no. Not my thing. I thought about it, but when I read this woman's account and she said it felt like her colon liquefied, I knew that jumping wasn't for me," she said.

"I've never been interested in jumping off a platform, either."

She smiled up at him, feeling more at peace with her decision not to do the jump than she had before.

"What were you doing this afternoon?"

"I met up with Jameson."

"Did you win big? How many games did you play today?" she asked, trying not to pry or ask about the woman's voice she'd heard earlier when they'd been on the phone.

"It wasn't a game. We had some drinks," he said, putting his hand on the center of her back as they walked into the hotel lobby. His touch was like a brand on her, and she struggled not to shiver under its warmth so low on her back.

"Did you have a chance to talk to Wendy?" he asked.

Good, let's talk, she thought. About anything, because she had to get outside of her own head.

"Yes. I really had a lot of fun with her."

"Didn't you expect to?" he asked. He drew her to a stop in the lobby out of the traffic path.

She wondered if he really cared so much about what she thought about shopping that he wanted to give her his full attention. She felt ridiculous that she cared that he might, but her ex-husband never listened to anything she said. In fact, he'd often walked so fast that she could barely keep up with him. It was beyond flattering to have a man pay attention to her the way Liam did.

"Shopping's never really been a leisure activity for me," she admitted. It was one of the things that her mom never let go of. She wanted Jane to go shopping with her whenever she went home for the weekend.

"I get the impression that it's more of a sport than a leisure activity to Wendy," Liam said.

"You have no idea. She's a fast walker, and I'm pretty sure we had at least ten pounds of merchandise in each hand."

"Did you get a chance to ask about Henry?"

"I did. She doesn't know if Henry's using again. And she was really reluctant to talk about her family's personal business." Jane didn't blame her. She'd felt like the worst sort of snoop asking all those questions.

"I'm sorry I put you in an awkward position," he said, leading the way across the lobby to the elevator bank.

The area was clear of people for once, and as soon as he pushed the call button, Liam drew her into his arms. "I missed you today."

She hugged him back, breathing his cologne along with the faint scent of cigar smoke. "We've only known each other a few days."

"I wish that mattered. But it doesn't seem to."

That did nothing to help her remember that he wasn't a forever kind of guy. Because deep inside she wanted him to be. She wanted him to be the kind of man she could ask a million questions. Actually, she wanted to have the right to ask him questions, and she was doing okay thinking she didn't have permission until he'd said that.

"Then maybe you can explain about the woman you were late to meet this morning?"

Liam dropped his arms and stepped back, scrubbing a

hand over his face. "That was just Didi. You've seen her before."

"The blonde?" This was more painful than it should be. He wasn't the first man to cheat on her. She'd thought she'd inured herself to the kind of pain that a man with a wandering eye could produce.

"Yes. It's not whatever you're obviously thinking it might be. She's just a friend. In fact, her boyfriend is here in Vegas with her."

"Then what were you doing with her?"

She saw the look in his eyes and knew he was going to give her another one of those half-answers that really told her absolutely nothing.

"Seriously, Liam, you can't say that this feels as if it doesn't matter how long we've known each other, and then give me a non-answer."

Each time it got easier and easier to pick the location of the fire and where he wanted to start it. This time his target was closer to the casinos. It was the only way he could be damned sure that he got the impact he wanted. It pissed him off. He'd tried to console himself with his usual addictions, but that had only served to agitate him more.

He needed to get back in control, and control these days was coming from only one source. Fire. He flicked the igniter on his lucky lighter and watched the flames dancing. He'd been behind the front desk again. Flirting with the clerks until they forgot he was there. As soon as they were busy checking in guests, he'd gone to one of the computers and logged in. Keyed himself a room key and then slowly disappeared.

He was concerned that the security tape would show him back there but had made sure to keep his back to the camera. Security concerns usually came from the other side of the front desk, so the cameras were trained on the guest side.

The lobby wasn't as crowded today as it had been a week ago, something he took an inordinate amount of pride in. No one had thought he could affect business in the casino but he saw the proof with his own eyes. Not as many people wanted to be in the cursed Royal Banner.

Edging his way through the lobby, he saw Liam O'Roarke and that pretty girl he was hanging out with. He'd never really liked Liam because he was so tight with Chase. Plus, lately he was always sticking his nose in where it didn't belong. Asking questions and talking to people he should know better than to talk to.

He'd heard from old Joe at the C&H that Liam had been asking questions over there after the fire. Questions that old Joe really should have known better than to answer. He wasn't a murderer, but if old Joe got hold of some bad dope and kicked it, he shrugged to himself, that was hardly his fault.

Fires were clean and left little in the way of evidence. Something that was becoming more and more important to him.

He entered the fourth-floor hallway, then took a can of hairspray from his bag and sprayed the camera casing pointed at the door. He moved carefully down the hall, making sure to keep out of range of the next camera. He sprayed that lens as well before opening the door to the room he'd gotten the key for. He'd picked a random room number, and this one was occupied but empty. There were souvenirs and an open suitcase on one of the beds, but the rest of the room was vacant. He threw the deadbolt and then went to work, carefully arranging the room the way he wanted it.

He cut holes in the walls on either side of the room. The room to the left was clearly vacant and he tossed his backpack in there, planning to use that for his escape. The other one was a mess. Whoever had been staying in that room had drunk the entire contents of the minibar and torn the hell out of the bed. There were five hundred-dollar bills on the nightstand along with a note that read "sorry about the mess."

He pocketed the money and then went to work getting the room ready to burn. He started the blaze there and then crawled back through the hole to the other room. It took a few minutes to get the flames burning there, and as he escaped into the last room, he heard the wail of the fire alarm as the sprinklers came on. He ran out into the hall with the other guests and merged with the crowd heading down the stairs and out of the building.

Liam knew that it was time to come clean with Jane but he couldn't talk to her about arson and the investigation while they were in the lobby. "Come back to my room and we can talk there."

"Why can't we talk here?"

"We can, but you want more than small talk," he said.

She nodded. "I get a little cranky sometimes."

"I didn't like seeing you with Henry the other night. I know that we'd just met and I really had no claim on you, but . . ."

She slipped her hand into his. "Okay, we can talk at your place."

The screeching of the fire alarm made Jane jump. Liam's pulse sped up and he was energized by the sound. He put his hand under Jane's elbow, urging her toward the doors that led outside, but not to the patio area because he wasn't sure where the fire was.

He needed to get her to safety first. It went against the grain, though, to leave the building when he knew there was a fire in there.

"What's going on?" Jane asked.

"Fire alarms."

"Maybe it's a prank," she said, and he heard the fear in her voice.

"Maybe. I want you to go straight out those doors and across the street. Don't stop. Understood?"

"Yes. But where will you be?"

"I'm going to stay close and see if I can help out."

"Maybe I can, too," she said.

No way in hell could he concentrate on the fire if Jane was anywhere near the building. He needed to know she was safe.

"Watch the building and see if you notice anyone acting oddly."

"Like what?" she asked. People were pouring into the lobby, a few of them panicking and running full-out for the door.

"Slow down," he said in a loud, firm voice. "Everyone walk. There's no reason to panic. The situation is under control."

And it was. Liam knew he could safely clear this lobby. Taking control of an emergency was what he'd been trained for since maturity.

"I wish you'd come with me."

"I can't leave if there's a chance I can help."

"Just because your dad taught you a few things when you were a kid doesn't mean—"

He put his hand over her mouth. "I'll be fine. You go out there and watch for anyone who's not behaving like the rest of the crowd."

"Like you?"

"Yes, but you know I didn't set the fire."

"Oh, do you think Chase will want to know if I see any-thing?"

"Definitely," he said, bending down to brush a kiss against her soft mouth. It was trembling a little, and her fear got to him. He shook his head as she walked away. He was invincible in this situation. He needed to believe it.

Doubts had no place in a fireman's mind when he was in the thick of an emergency. The lobby emptied quickly as the Las Vegas firefghters started entering the building. Liam raced to his bungalow and donned the turn-out gear that he'd had his brother-in-law ship out to him. Then he reentered the building.

Liam identified himself to the officer in charge, Crew Chief Danner.

"What have we got here?"

"Smoke pouring down from the fourth floor. I've got two teams upstairs. I can talk to you about the arson investigation after we get the fire under control."

"I can help. I'm a career firefighter from South Dade. More than twenty years on the engine. You can always use another pair of hands."

"True, but I need a pair of hands my guys can trust."

"I understand, but I don't want to walk away and wait this out."

"Stay with me. If we need you, I'll send you up."

Five minutes later a firefighter came back down toward the chief. "My air mask is out of oxygen."

Liam narrowed his gaze on the man. That was a sign of a defective mask or sloppiness on the firefighter's part. And since getting clear air was paramount to survival, sloppy firefighters usually didn't last long.

"You still ready to go, O'Roarke?"

"Yes, sir."

"You can take Stevens's place on the fourth floor."

Stevens handed Liam his radio and Liam quickly put it on. He could hear the men upstairs fighting the blaze reporting down to the captain.

Liam made his way up the stairs, taking them two at a time. When he got to the floor he followed the fire hose, which was stretched from the stairwell down the long corridor. The doors to the rooms were all opened. Thick smoke made visibility difficult, but Liam was used to these circumstances. Debris fell from the fire-damaged roof.

Liam noted that the smoke was a normal color, indicating that at first glance the fire was not a chemical one.

He didn't think about the dangers inherent in his job—this was what he'd trained a lifetime for. This was so much more satisfying than a damned arson investigation.

Liam helped the rest of the firefighters battle the blaze and in a short time they had it under control. There was a lot of cursing amongst them, but only after the danger had passed.

A feeling of camaraderie flowed among the firefighters, and Liam felt comfortable despite the fact that he'd never met them before.

"You're always welcome on my crew, O'Roarke," Chief Danner said.

"Thanks, man," Liam said as he left the crew. He knew he needed to find Jane and make some excuse, then find Didi so they could go over the scene.

Liam walked up and down the hallway. "Where was the point of origin?"

"Looks like either room 412 or 414."

Liam went into 412 and found the same thing they'd noticed on the unoccupied floor two days ago. That weird hole cut in the wall.

As soon as Didi arrived they both started taking notes—a pattern was definitely developing. And their arsonist was getting impatient, Liam thought. The time between each fire was getting shorter and shorter, the blazes more intense and more dangerous to the guests staying at the Royal Banner.

After forty-five minutes, Jane was a nervous wreck waiting for Liam to come out of the casino. She'd been watching the crowd, looking for anyone who appeared to be doing anything untoward, but her worry for Liam took most of her concentration.

She'd never known anyone who worked in any kind of emergency situation like this one. She wondered if he was a volunteer firefighter when he wasn't gambling. It would make sense, given his background.

"What's going on?" Henry asked, coming up beside her. His hair was disheveled. She looked closely at his eyes, trying to see if they were dilated, but in the dark it was difficult to make it out.

"Another fire—I don't know much more than that. The alarm went off almost an hour ago."

"Were you inside again?"

"Yes. I'm beginning to think I would be better off staying somewhere else."

"I'd have to agree," Henry said. "Don't tell my brother I said that."

"I won't," she said.

Henry kept staring at the building. The flames were out and the smoke wasn't pouring out the way it had been earlier but it lingered in the air. The scent was thick and pungent, stinging her nose.

"I think this is a record number of fires. Have you seen Chase?" Henry asked.

"No . . . I think he's out of town."

Henry flushed. "That's right—I'd forgotten."

She patted his arm. "There's been a lot of excitement. Were you in the casino when the alarms went off?"

"No," Henry said. "I wasn't. I'm going to go see if I can find out what's going on."

Henry left and Jane noticed Jameson and his entourage standing a few feet away. They were complaining loudly about the service they'd received and about the inconvenience of not being able to start their tournament game.

She saw the firefighters start emerging from the building and searched for Liam's tall frame amongst the men in their turn-out gear and helmets, but didn't see him. She took her phone out of her purse and dialed his number.

"O'Roarke."

"It's Jane. Where are you? Are you okay?" It was a relief to hear his voice. The images she'd had of him somehow trapped in a smoke-and-fire-filled hallway disappeared.

"Yes, baby, I'm fine. I'll be downstairs in a few minutes."

"Good, I was beginning to worry when I saw the firefighters come out and still no sign of you," she said. Her earlier debate about what he meant to her suddenly seemed trivial and she knew now that vacation fling or not, she cared for Liam. That might not be what she was supposed to do but that was something she couldn't change about herself .

She heard voices in the background on his phone. "Where are you?"

"At the fire scene—I figured I should get a good look so I can tell Chase exactly what happened. But I'm working my way outside."

"Won't the crew chief or fire marshal give Chase a report?"

"Yes, you're right, they will. Are you still across the street?"

"Yes," she said. "I'm near the monorail entrance."

"The platform or street level?"

"Street level," she said. "The crowd is huge out here."

"Did you see anyone acting suspicious?"

"I'm not really sure what you mean," she said.

"Did you see anyone who wasn't concerned about their safety?"

"Your gambler friend was complaining really loudly that the service stunk at this casino since tonight's poker tournament was being delayed."

"Jameson?"

"Yes. He had a large group of people with him, so maybe he was just making noise to impress his friends."

"He is a bit of a blowhard," Liam said, coming up behind her. He wrapped his arm around her waist and she turned around so she could hug him back.

She'd never been so happy to see him before. She was glad that he was out of the building and back with her.

"I thought Jameson was your friend," she said, forcing herself to drop her arms and step back. She was jostled by a man in the crowd trying to get around them.

"That doesn't make me blind to his faults," Liam said, pulling her back to his side. "Let's get out of the crowd."

"Can we return to the hotel?"

"Not for a few more hours. Let's go get something to eat."

Jane felt exhausted by all that had happened. She'd started her vacation fling, butted into a stranger's personal business, almost did something death-defying, and then faced her second fire. She sighed.

"What's the matter?"

"Vegas is a little too exciting for me."

"Everything in Vegas?" he asked.

She glanced up at him and knew she wouldn't trade anything for the chance to have met him. She didn't like the danger of the fires in the hotel but she did like the fact that they had brought her to Liam.

Chapter 16

Liam opened the door to the bungalow and glanced inside. "I've been a bachelor for a long time. Give me a minute to pick up my mess."

"Take your time," she said, sitting down on one of the chairs to the left of the door. The evening was chilly but not cold, and after the roller-coaster day they'd had, that suited her just fine.

She stared up at the stars and angled her head so she could see the moon. It was the three-quarter one. She extended her arm like she used to when she was little, putting her thumb over the moon.

"What are you doing?" Liam asked as he returned.

"Playing hide-and-seek with the moon."

"Why don't you come and play with me instead?" He scooped her up off the chair and carried her into the bungalow. No man had ever carried her over the threshold before. Rodney had been afraid of dropping her.

She clutched at his shoulders as he carried her. They hadn't talked about anything too heavy at dinner, and a part of her was disappointed. But after the scare earlier this evening with the fire and her fear for him, she really just wanted this. Wanted to be in his arms and feel him pressed up against her.

He lowered his head to hers as he put her on her feet.

182 / Katherine Garbera

The small living room was lit from the lights in the bedroom and a large, industrial-strength flashlight was on in one corner for illumination.

"What is that?"

"I didn't have any candles and I wanted some mood lighting."

She laughed at him. "You're all the mood enhancement I need."

He waggled his eyebrows at her. "Ah, you say the nicest things."

"I do, don't I?"

"How about putting those words to action?" he asked, rubbing his finger against the side of her neck right over her frantically beating pulse.

"How?"

"Well, we did talk about strip clubs the other night . . ."

Jane pretended to think it over to cover her own nervousness. She'd never played any kind of bedroom games before and it was clear that he wanted to.

"No pressure, baby," he said.

"Okay, but you're going to have to do something for me."

"Just say the word and I'm yours."

She wished he were really hers. But for tonight he was, and she was ready to embrace this experience and this man.

The lighting was dim enough to make her feel more comfortable than she would have if she'd been standing in the fully lit room.

"Take off your shirt," she said.

"I thought you were the one who'd be removing your clothes."

"Your incredible chest will inspire me."

"Incredible, eh? I like the sound of that."

"I can't be the first woman who ever said that."

"You're the only woman whose opinion matters," he said. He unbuttoned his shirt slowly and then drew it off, tossing it over the back of the chair. Then he pulled her into his arms and kissed her. He thrust his tongue deep in her mouth. She felt the rekindling of her own desire. She wanted him again. She tried to angle her head to reciprocate as he held her still.

"I want to make sure you're properly inspired."

"Oh, I am," she said. "Go sit down."

She felt a little foolish now that he was sitting there watching her, but the fire in his eyes eased her a little. "There isn't any music."

"I've got some speakers for my iPod," he said. He went over to the desk area and picked up the MP3 player, then set it in the speaker system. "I've got 'Sweet Jane' by the Velvet Underground or 'Jane' by Barenaked Ladies."

Songs that had her name in them . . . "Were you planning this?"

"Maybe."

"Um . . . I only know the Barenaked Ladies one," she said, kicking off her shoes.

"Slow and sexy it is," he said.

Soon the music started playing and she still stood there kind of awkwardly, but when her eyes met his she saw how sexy he thought she was. She started to sway to the music and he sank back down in the chair as she slowly danced around him.

He had a nice baritone voice and he sang along with the chorus. Just her name over and over again. She slowly pulled her blouse up over her head and kept dancing around him. Now in only her bra and jeans, she ran her hand down the center of her sternum and watched his eyes narrow.

He mirrored her movements, stroking his hand down his own chest. She bent down over him and kissed his four-leaf clover.

She stepped back when he would have touched her and unfastened the button at the top of her jeans, then lowered the zipper and shimmied out of them. She turned her back to him as she bent down to free her legs.

She let her hips sway to the beat and tossed her hair as she stood up and turned back to face him.

She danced closer to him, reaching between her breasts for the front clasp of her bra and unfastening it. She peeled the cups away from her breasts for a quick second and then drew the fabric back over herself.

"Jane."

"What?"

"Stop teasing me."

"I thought it was called a strip*tease*."

"Well, in a club maybe but here . . . I'm going to have you, baby."

"Are you?"

"Yes, I am," he said, getting to his feet. He closed the distance between them.

As he lifted her in his arms, she wrapped her legs around his hips. Suddenly the dynamics changed between them.

This was his embrace and he totally dominated her. The music changed to The Velvet Underground's "Sweet Jane" and he swayed with the beat.

"You're mine," he said, taking the strap of her bra in one hand and pulling it down and off her body.

"Yours?"

She found the proof she was searching for that Liam was different from every other man she'd ever met.

Her nipples tightened and her breasts felt too full as he danced them around the living room, the ridge of his erection bumping against the very center of her. She moaned deep in her throat and shifted against him.

His biceps flexed as he shifted her in his arms and sat back down in the chair. She let her legs fall on either side of his hips, straddling him.

He ran his hands all over her body; his mouth moved

down the column of her neck, nibbling and biting softly. He lingered at the base of her neck where she knew her pulse beat frantically. Everything in her body clenched. Not enough to push her over the edge, just enough to make her hungry—frantic for more of him. She rocked her hips against him.

Jane scored his shoulders with her fingernails and when he moaned her name, she knew he liked it. She skimmed the edge of her nails down his chest, tracing the outline of the clover again and again. She was so glad he had a good-luck charm to keep him safe, because he lived his life without regard to the consequences.

He wrapped his arms around her body, pulling her closer as his mouth found hers again. She liked the way she was surrounded by him. Felt very feminine as she was cradled in his arms. His skin was hot to the touch and she wrapped her arms around his body, pulling him closer.

He pulled back, staring down at her. Then he traced one finger over the full globes of her breasts. She shifted her shoulders, waiting for his caress. He took one of her nipples between his thumb and forefinger, pinching lightly.

She reached between their bodies, unfastening his pants and freeing his erection. His mouth fastened on her left nipple, suckling her strongly. She undulated against him, lifting her hips toward him. He drew his other hand down her body under the fabric of her tiny ice-blue panties, his fingers tangling in the hair at her center.

He caressed her between her legs until she was frantically holding his head to her breasts, trying to find her release, but it remained just out of her reach. She skimmed her hands down his body, caressing his hip bone, and then moving her fingers around to his cock.

His breath hissed out as she reached between his legs, but the fabric of his pants was in her way. She pushed herself off his lap.

"Take your pants off."

"Yes," was all he said. He pushed the jeans and his underwear to the floor and kicked them away. She stripped off her panties and turned back to him.

"There's a condom in the nightstand," he said.

"Stay here, I'll be right back." She returned a moment later with the condom—she tossed it to Liam and fell to her knees between his legs. She wanted a chance to explore.

"Jane, baby, you're killing me."

She liked the sound of that, and the way his breath caught whenever she scored his sac with her nails.

"Put it on me."

"With pleasure."

She opened the package before she remembered she hadn't done this before, but it wasn't that hard to figure out. She placed it on his tip and then rolled it down his hard length. When he groaned deep in his throat, she thought maybe she'd done it right.

She started to reach lower again but he caught her hand and stretched it over her head, drawing her to her feet and back down on his lap.

He shifted his body underneath her, using one hand to probe at the entrance of her body before she felt the whole, hard length of him.

But he made no move to take her. She looked up at him. "You're mine."

She couldn't respond to that.

"I . . ."

"Watch me take you, Jane."

He thrust inside her then. Lifting her up, holding her with his big hands on her butt as he repeatedly drove into her. He went deeper than he had the last time they'd made love. She felt too full, stretched and surrounded by him.

He bit her neck carefully and sucked against her skin and everything tightened inside her until she felt her climax spread through her body. Her skin was pulsing, her body tightening around his plunging cock. A minute later he came.

She rested her head on his shoulder and held him. "I guess I can understand why you like exotic dancing."

"Only if the dancer is you, Jane."

Liam's phone rang in the middle of the night—he stretched his arm out to get it, trying not to disturb Jane. When he saw on the caller ID that it was Chase, he knew he had to take it.

He eased out of bed and walked into the other room. "O'Roarke here."

"I just landed and got news that we had another fire. What the hell is going on?"

"Did you get the details on the fire yet? We're still processing the scene so I don't have too much to go on yet." He rubbed his hand over his eyes, trying to wake up. Normally he didn't mind middle-of-the-night calls. Hell, in all his years as a firefighter he'd been awakened more times than he could count. But he'd wanted to stay in bed and hold Jane all night long.

"Fuck that, Liam. I want answers."

"Well . . . is Henry using again?" That was his main concern right now. Until they had some answers about Henry he couldn't move him off the list of suspects.

"What does that have to do with the fires?"

"It puts him at the top of my suspects list if he is," Liam said. He found his jeans on the floor and stepped into them before sitting down in the chair he'd made love to Jane in. God, she was a complication he hadn't been expecting.

"Damn, I have no idea what he's been up to. He was gambling in my casinos using house credit for the last few months but he recently started losing and I cut off his funds."

"Well, that might be a motive as far as Henry is concerned. The main thing that bothers me about him as a suspect is that I don't think he's organized enough to plan this."

Chase didn't say anything for a few minutes, and Liam could hear the sounds of Mozart drifting through the line. "Where are you?"

"At my hotel in Monaco. But I'm going to be heading back to Vegas as soon as the jet is refueled. Henry can be very organized once he focuses on something. When I get back I'll talk to him."

"Okay. We'll probably have a more complete picture of the last fire by then."

"Is that all?"

"No—we came across a fire at your Atlantic City casino some fifteen years ago. What can you tell me about that?"

"Not much. Dad was still running things then. I think it was a disgruntled employee."

"Do you have any records from back then? The fire departments aren't computerized yet."

"I'm not sure. I'll check into it for you. I don't think this is related. I mean, Henry wasn't even out of school then."

"He's not our only suspect."

"Did you talk to Jameson?"

"Yes. I still couldn't pin him down. He hates you and he's honest about that, but he does like the life he has now."

"Yeah, that's thanks to me and the fact that I bought out his crappy hotel."

Liam rubbed his hand over his chest, feeling the faint marks left by Jane's fingernails. "That's what he said."

"I'm on a short fuse tonight, sorry. No sleep and all that."

"You can't offend me—you know that."

Chase laughed. "That's true. Wendy told me she went shopping with Jane today. You serious about her?"

Liam didn't want to get into that with Chase or, really,

anyone else. He hadn't figured out what was going on between him and Jane yet. He knew that she was a thirst that wasn't easy to quench. He wanted to be with her all the time.

"Yeah, I think I am."

Chase whistled long and low. "Never thought I'd see the day."

Liam, either. And he didn't want to think about the fact that he was thinking about giving up his single life for Jane. Especially since she was determined that he was just a vacation fling. God, he wanted more than a vacation with her, but how was he going to convince her that she did, too?

He was good at walking away and not so good at sticking around.

"Back to the investigation. Didi said she talked to one of the kids who works in the kitchen at the C&H. She's pretty sure he saw something the night of the fire that consumed the wedding chapel, but he's afraid to talk."

"Why would he be afraid unless he's hiding something?" Chase said.

"It's a normal reaction. Most people don't like to be labeled a snitch and prefer to mind their own business. Especially this kid. He's young and doesn't speak English."

"What do you want me to do?"

"Well, I know your head chef runs that place like a general and his staff really respects him. I was hoping you could have him talk to the kid."

"Sure. I'll talk to him as soon as he gets in today," Chase said. "Is there anything else?"

"Well, you'll be happy to know that you are no longer a suspect and we don't think you set the fires for financial gain."

"Yeah, that's a relief."

Chase hung up and Liam stayed in the chair. He didn't feel anything close to relief and he wouldn't until they stopped whoever was setting the fires. At the same time, he wanted the investigation over with so he could concentrate on Jane.

Jane heard the sound of Liam's voice and rolled over. He had such a deep, rich voice that she liked the sound of it. She wondered if he'd read to her in bed. That had been something she'd tried to get Rodney to do when it was clear they lacked intimacy, but he wasn't interested and said it made him feel stupid.

In the end she was the one who was stupid, because she'd worked so hard to try to make herself into someone he'd care about enough to make the big, romantic gestures.

She felt confident that Liam would do it if she asked him to, just because she asked. And he'd never worry about seeming foolish because that just wasn't the way he was built. The bed was empty and the only light in the room came from the moon shining in through the window. A quick glance at her watch showed that it was almost three.

She got out of bed and looked around for something to put on. She found one of Liam's shirts hanging in the closet and donned that.

"Did I wake you?" Liam asked, coming back into the bedroom.

"Yeah, but I'm not a sound sleeper." At home she woke to the slightest sound. Her college years had been a nightmare due to all the noise, but she'd met Rodney her junior year and they'd gotten an apartment off campus, which had been nice for a while.

"Me, either. Actually I'm a bit of an insomniac," Liam said. "I think it's because my old man was always running drills around the house. Waking us in the middle of the night and seeing how quickly we could get out of the house."

Her heart ached at the thought of Liam as a little boy waking to that kind of situation. "Did you like that?"

He shrugged. "It was okay. One of the perks of that kind of upbringing is that I'm always prepared. I wake up quickly and react swiftly."

"I'm not like that."

"No reason for you to be," he said.

"I usually need a solid eight hours every night but it's harder to sleep here. Everything's always going, you know?" Jane asked.

"Yeah, I do."

"That's part of the appeal of it all. Vegas is a place out of time, out of our real lives."

What did he mean? Was he trying to tell her that this was it? What he had to offer her was the vacation affair and nothing more?

"I do understand the need to escape," she said softly, sitting on the bed. "But in the end we always come back to ourselves."

"Yeah, we do. Have you figured yourself out yet, Jane?"

"Almost," she said, realizing that her affair with Liam had shown her things about herself she'd never seen before. She was a sensuous woman, something she'd never have guessed during her marriage. And she liked sex—something else that was new.

"Good. I think you have a solid core to who you are, but you're afraid to let anyone see that."

There was more than an element of truth in what he said. "You should be a therapist."

"What can I say? I've had a lot of experience diagnosing other people's problems."

Was he a bartender? He didn't say anything else but came into the room and sat down on the bed next to her, piling pillows up behind his back and shifting around until he was comfortable.

"Come up here by me."

She shifted around so she was lying on her side next to him.

"Is everything okay with your family?"

"Yes. It was . . . just a call about some business."

"You've never said exactly what it is you do," she said, trying not to expect too much from this moment.

"Baby, I don't want to talk about that."

"Are you a firefighter? Is that why you don't want to talk about it?"

"Why do you think that?"

"It's clear to me you have some training in that area, just from the way you've reacted to the two fires we've been in."

"Yeah, I've had some training," he said, rubbing his hand down her back. He pulled her closer to his chest. Wrapped in his heavy arms, her cheek resting over his heart, she wondered if he was running away from who he was at home . . . the same way she had.

"Are you burned out? Did you see something so horrific it made you question what you wanted in life? You can talk to me."

His arms tightened around her and he didn't say anything for a long time. "You are the sweetest gift I've ever received."

She wasn't sure what that meant. "You are the best part of this vacation."

"Good. I didn't know the old Jane but I like the woman you are."

"Old Jane . . . you wouldn't have looked twice at her."

He gave her a candid look and ran his hand up under her shirt. "I'm pretty sure I would have noticed you no matter what."

"Well, I would have been too afraid to talk to you."

"Afraid of what?"

"I don't know. It's just, you're so handsome and I'm just . . . plain Jane."

He took her face in both of his hands. "You are not plain, Jane. You are incandescent in the way you try new things and the way you . . . I don't know, but there's a light inside you that draws people to you."

She wanted to say something to him but had no words. He didn't give her a chance to ask him any more questions. Instead he pulled her more fully into his embrace, making love to her until she came so hard that she drifted off to sleep.

Chapter 17

Jane stood in the back of the hotel suite they'd rented for the press junket for *Dirty Vegas*. The room was set up in convenient conversation areas, each one backed with pipe and draping and the promotional poster for the movie. She had the director Raine Rivers, who had also co-written the screenplay with her movie-star husband. It was based loosely on the story of him and three of his friends from his twenties.

"Thanks for talking me into the road trip," Eva said. She had a bottle of Evian in one hand and her press credentials in the other. "That was one hell of an exclusive."

"You're welcome." *Backstage Hollywood* had devoted most of their airtime to running the road trip with Eva. It was a great publicity boon. She was only hoping that the guys stayed clean and sober, at least while they were in the limelight.

The room wasn't filled with reporters yet. This morning they were doing a satellite up-link. Each of the actors was doing about fifteen different morning shows in several key markets.

Jane signaled Mitchell to come and handle Eva. She liked her but didn't have time to chat this morning.

"Eva, this is Mitchell—he works in my office. He's going to give you some talking points on the director."

Jane moved away from them. She'd realized the key to not thinking about Liam and the way he never answered any of the questions she put to him about his life was to keep moving. The busier she was, the less time she had to dwell on the fact that she was falling in love with a man who really did think of her as a vacation lover.

He might occasionally say something different, but she saw the truth in his evasions. A woman who he was only going to know on vacation didn't need the details of his life or his career.

Yet she'd shared those things with him. Shared all those personal details that would have been too embarrassing to tell anyone else.

"Everything is running smoothly," Josef said when she approached him. "Thanks for all your hard work pulling this together."

"That's what you pay me for."

"Well, right now I believe we're paying you to be on vacation."

"I'm only working six hours a day . . . that *is* a vacation."

He laughed and they chatted about Vegas before one of the bigwigs for the Royal Banner hotel came over to make sure they didn't need anything else. Jane left the ballroom because she simply wasn't needed there. Everything was running smoothly and Mitchell needed this moment to make a good impression on Josef.

She wandered around the mezzanine before realizing she wasn't exactly aimless. She knew where she wanted to go. She stopped in front of the tattoo parlor.

Standing there in the doorway, she knew she wanted a permanent reminder of her time in Vegas. Something that she'd always have to remember this trip and the changes she'd made.

She opened the door before she could change her mind.

"I remember you," the man with the gauge earring said.

"I'm Jane."

"Sterno."

She wanted to ask a million questions about that name but decided they were probably better left unsaid.

"Are you just looking again?"

She shrugged. "I'm not sure."

"What aren't you sure about?"

The blood and the pain, she thought. But she'd had her pain already when her marriage and the safe life she'd built for herself had fallen apart and now she wanted something to celebrate who she'd become.

"Is it painful?"

"Not too bad. Feels like a light stinging," Sterno said. "Right, Chuck?"

The man Sterno was working on glanced up. "Yeah, not bad at all. This is my third one."

Chuck was getting a tattoo band around his left arm.

"Kallie?" Sterno called.

A petite redhead came up from the back. "Jane's thinking about getting ink done."

"Cool. Come on over here and I'll talk you through our process."

Jane felt less nervous now that she was in here. Kallie pulled out a pad of paper. And Jane took out her credit card before she could change her mind.

"Okay, fill out the top part here," she said, drawing a line that covered the first half of the page. "Then you can look through the books over there with the designs in them or . . . did you bring your own design?"

She hadn't but she knew what she wanted. A four-leaf clover. She hadn't been planning on it until this moment but it was exactly what she wanted.

"I want a clover."

"We've got some in the book or one of our artists can sketch an original design for you. That'll be extra."

She didn't mind. One thing about having spent her entire life being a good girl was that she'd saved almost every penny she'd ever made. She'd put a dent in that savings when she'd redone her image and wardrobe, but she still had plenty for a high-end tattoo.

Liam stood up to stretch. His back ached from sitting for four hours in a desk chair that was really too small for his six-five frame. He was almost cross-eyed from reviewing all the security tape.

But they were making headway. The first fire had nothing but a shadowy blur of a figure running down a darkened hallway. Fires two and three also had the blurry figure, and it took a while to figure out that the arsonist had sprayed something on the cameras.

The fourth one had nothing because the unoccupied floor where the renovation was taking place hadn't been wired with cameras yet. He rubbed the back of his neck, looking at the tape of the previous night. He saw Jane emerge from her room and in the smoky hallway saw her confusion and panic.

He froze the frame on her and reached out to touch the screen. He'd hated waking up alone, but she'd left him a note . . . something he'd done to her, and he realized he didn't like that. A note wasn't good enough after a night filled with soul-sex.

"Find anything?"

"Well, the fifth fire seems to be a bit of an anomaly. The arsonist was definitely using something on the cameras, but in this case the cameras on the twenty-fifth floor were fogged up but he didn't end up starting the fire there."

"That was the one in the wedding chapel?"

"Yeah. I think something spooked him."

"And he turned his attention to a different target?"

"It's the only thing that makes sense." Liam rolled his shoulders and sat back down. He pulled up the images from the wedding fire. The door to the antechamber opened and a bit of flame licked out into the hallway as the arsonist appeared. He was looking down and the billowy smoke obscured any chance they had to really see his face as he sprinted down the hall.

"Did you talk to the dishwasher? What's his name, Juan?" Didi asked.

"Yes, Juan and I also chatted with the head chef, Everett. Thanks for setting that up."

"No problem. What'd they say?" Liam said.

"He saw . . ." Didi picked up her notebook. "A Caucasian man about five-ten. The man entered the kitchens from the service hallway and was watching his back as he walked through. Juan said the man looked over at him, narrowed his eyes, and kept on walking."

"Would he recognize the suspect if he saw him again?"

Didi shrugged. "I have no idea. He was nervous just talking to me."

"Did he have any other description? Hair color, eye color?"

"Brown hair and green eyes."

"Well, that really narrows things down," Liam said sarcastically.

"Joe in the alleyway saw a dark-haired man running from the scene."

"Our arsonist got a little sloppy on this one," Didi said.

"Yes, he did."

"What about the fire last night?"

"The tapes aren't here yet," Liam said. "But I have noticed that he's getting closer and closer to the casinos. I wondered if that's his intention."

"Could be. He's starting the fires right on top of each other. At first . . . at first he was cooling out and building back up to starting a blaze. Now his downtime is being shortened."

"So something else is involved," Liam said.

"I think we have to go with revenge or simply vandalism."

"Me, too. Where's the suspect list?"

Didi pushed her pad across the table toward him. The list had been narrowed until the only three left were Jameson Bradley, Henry Banner, and Chase Banner. All three men had similar coloring and were about the same height. They matched Juan's description.

"To be honest, I can't see Chase doing this," Liam said. There had been that note of sheer frustration in Chase's voice when they'd spoken on the phone. "He doesn't need this kind of aggravation. Do you have a motive for him?"

"No. But he has availability to the main security room and the alarms."

"Anything else?" Liam asked.

"No. Not really."

"Let's cross him off. The last fire took place when he wasn't even here."

"We don't have proof of that yet," Didi said.

"I've asked Sonic Speed—the corporate jet company he uses—to send over a flight plan for the trip to Europe."

"Good. Once we have it, he's off the list. Who's next, Jameson or Henry?"

"Both men know this hotel and the C&H like the back of their hands," Liam said.

"Jameson hates Chase. He might put on a friendly face when he's in the casino, but I have several eye witness reports of his behavior after the fire. He made inappropriate comments, and after the last one, started laughing, saying . . ." Didi flipped through the papers in front of her. "'Banner will have a hard time keeping things going if this keeps up.'"

Liam stood up and paced around the room. "That's not an expression of guilt."

"You have to admit he sounds like he's got an ax to grind where Chase is concerned."

Yeah, it did sound that way. "How does he compare to Henry?"

"We haven't had Henry at any of the actual post-fire crowds. In fact, when I talked to him it seemed he wasn't even in the Banner hotels during the fires."

"Did you believe him?" Liam asked.

"He wasn't telling me everything but I'm not really sure what he was lying about."

Liam rubbed his forehead. "The leads in this investigation suck."

"No, they don't. You just want a clear-cut picture of who it is, and we don't have it yet," Didi said.

His cell phone rang, indicating he had a new e-mail. He glanced down at the screen. "Finally."

"What is it?"

"The crime scene evidence has been processed."

He opened the file and read it quickly. Seemed that some of the charred cloth they'd collected was very similar. "Backpacks. He's carrying his accelerants to the fires in a backpack."

"Make and model?"

"I'm forwarding it to you. Our guys even sent a list of where they can be purchased in this zip code."

"I'll hit the stores later after lunch."

"Want to grab a bite together?"

Didi blushed and glanced away. "I can't. I have plans."

"Plans? Or a date?"

"Leave it alone, O'Roarke."

"Ah, so it *is* a date. With the forensic accountant?"

"Yes, if you must know. It is with Tod."

"Good, you need something other than work in your life."

"So do you," she said.

She left before he could respond to that, and Liam absently rubbed a hand over his chest. He did have someone in his life who meant more to him than his job. The only question was, how was he going to keep her?

The text-message from Shanna had been short and to the point, asking Jane to meet her outside the main casino. Jane gingerly replaced the Saran Wrap and Vaseline combo that covered the tattoo on her left hip. It was tender but the process hadn't been painful.

She changed into a loose-fitting skirt and halter top and a pair of high-heeled sandals. She fluffed up her short hair and as she leaned close to the mirror to reapply her lip gloss, she realized for the first time she felt like she was wearing her own clothes. That she wasn't dressing up and pretending to be someone else.

She left the room, carrying only a small handbag and her cell phone. The lobby was crowded for the first time in days.

"What's going on?" Jane asked Shanna as she approached her.

"Some kind of big poker game. The stakes have risen into the six-figure area. I guess the game has been going on for a few hours, so word got out." Shanna looked like her usually sultry self, but for once Jane realized she didn't feel like Shanna's plain friend. She smiled inwardly, enjoying her new confidence. God knew it was about time.

"Who's playing?" she asked, absently scanning the lobby

for Liam. She had almost called him but had chickened out at the last second . . . where was her confidence with him?

"Bradley something and a few other guys. Wanna check it out?"

"Ah, yes," she said. Was Liam in there gambling his life away, she wondered. It was difficult to get close enough to the velvet ropes, but Shanna pushed her way through the crowd, keeping one hand on Jane's wrist. Soon the two of them were standing at the front. Liam was indeed at the table, along with Henry Banner, Jameson Bradley, and two other players she didn't recognize.

The men looked stiff and serious as they each contemplated their cards. She realized she was seeing a different side to Liam than she had before. Even when they'd been in the fire, she hadn't seen this kind of . . . dead calm.

"Isn't that the guy you've been hanging out with?" Shanna asked, pointing toward the table.

"Yes, that's Liam," she said. Liam and Henry sat next to each other. Henry wasn't as stoic as Liam. As each card was dealt to the man, Jane saw him react. Just a little tightening around his eyes.

"The blond?"

"Yes," she said, resenting the fact that Shanna was talking. She wanted to soak in the details as he sat at the table. This was his poker face, she realized.

"You know the other guy, too, right?" Shanna asked.

"Henry? Yes. He's the one who taught me to play twenty-one." But the cool, calm guy who'd told her that gambling was in his blood had lost his ease. Tension simmered in the air, and not just around Henry.

"Well, you're running with the big guys. Not bad for someone who doesn't like to gamble," Shanna said.

She shook her head, realizing that she'd been gambling with her life. Gambling with her future happiness, trying so hard to insulate herself from pain and taking a risk on Liam. He glanced up and flashed her a smile.

She returned it, thinking that maybe . . . just maybe, this risk was going to pay off. It didn't matter that she'd never really thought that he could be the man for her. Suddenly she knew he was. She didn't have to worry or pretend that she was falling in love with him.

She *was* in love with him.

A stranger. A man she knew precious little about. That didn't matter. She knew him in ways she couldn't possibly explain, but her heart understood.

"Jane?"

"What?"

"I asked if you were going to stay here and watch or if you wanted to go play?"

"I'm going to stay here," she said. She wanted to be near Liam.

"I'm going to split. Is that okay with you?"

"Yeah, go ahead. I'll catch up with you later."

"I'll be around, probably playing the slots. I'm feeling lucky tonight."

"You go, girl."

Shanna gave her a quick hug and walked away. Jane wished she'd worn a pair of flats, as her feet began to hurt. When the hand ended, Liam pushed away from the table and walked toward her.

He unhooked the velvet rope and reached for her, wrapping one big hand around her hips and drawing her close to him. He leaned down and brushed his lips over hers. Just a light touch—mouth-to-mouth, but she felt it all the way to her soul.

"I missed you today," he said against her skin.

She wrapped her arms around his shoulders leaning against him. "I missed you, too."

She felt the eyes of the other watchers on the two of

them. But that didn't matter. For the first time in her life she felt free, deep inside where she'd always kept herself on a tight rein, never letting anyone see anything important to her.

But she wanted Liam and the world to know that she was a different woman now and that she was claiming her man.

Chapter 18

Liam tucked Jane under his shoulder and led her away from the ropes and back to the table. "You can sit on my lap and be my good-luck charm."

"Ha. I know professionals don't put stock in luck," she said carefully. She was curious what he'd done all day but didn't want to ask. She was playing a silly game in her head, acting as if he told her without her prompting, it would lend credence to what he said.

"How do you know that?" he asked, keeping his arm around her.

She felt safe tucked up against his side like she belonged with him. That sense of belonging felt new, like her confidence did. As if she'd finally found a place where she fit in, that elusive place she'd been searching for.

"I bought a book in the gift shop this morning and it said that pros are savvy players," she said. She wanted to understand more of what she knew about Liam. After reading the book this afternoon she understood that maybe he was hiding part of his life from her because he wanted her to only see a successful gambler.

"That's true," he said. "But you can still sit on my lap."

She tried not to feel disappointed at his joking. Knew that that was the way he dealt with life. His easy-going manner and his smile hid the man she'd had glimpses of during the

208 / Katherine Garbera

night. Only when they were both naked and making love did she feel like she had a quick look at the real man.

"Forget it," she said, striving for a lightness she didn't feel. "I don't want to distract you during a big game. Why have you all stopped?"

"One of the players needed to see the banker about more funds," he said, nodding toward the farthest corner behind the table.

"Henry?" she asked easily, recognizing him.

"Yes."

"Is he independently wealthy? He told me he doesn't work, just lives his life."

Liam laughed. "That sounds like Henry. I don't know much about his finances. I think Chase supports him some. I know he does here in the casinos."

"That's got to chafe a little bit," Jane said.

"What? Letting Chase support him?"

"Yes. I hope that I didn't mess things up for him when I mentioned his odd behavior to Wendy."

"He hasn't been acting weird today. Maybe you just caught him on an off day," Liam said.

"God, I hope so," she said, nibbling on her lower lip. "I feel bad I said anything to Wendy."

"Don't worry about it. Chase keeps a close eye on Henry, anyway."

"Why is that?"

"Just the way of big brothers."

"And big sisters," Jane added. "I always tried to look out for Marcus but he's his own person and does his own thing."

"My siblings are like that, too. The thing with Henry and Chase is that Henry has never stood on his own. And Chase is one of those guys who kind of encouraged Henry to lean on him."

Henry said something profane and loud. Jane glanced

over at him where he was talking to another gentleman. "What's going on?"

"No clue," Liam said.

Jameson left the bar where he'd been getting a drink and walked over to Henry.

Whatever he said made Henry angry, and the other man turned, knocking Jameson's glass so that the drink spilled down his arm.

"I'm out of here," Henry said, walking out of the roped-off area. He shoved his way past the bouncer, and disappeared into the crowd.

"That doesn't look good," Jane said.

"No, it doesn't," Liam agreed.

"Should I go after him?" Jane asked.

"Nah, let him cool off. He's been losing all day. It was just a matter of time before the bank cut him off."

Jane shook her head. Why would anyone keep playing when things were clearly not going their way? "How are you doing?"

"Worried?"

"Should I be?"

"I'm not going to storm out of here anytime soon," he said.

"I'm glad to hear that."

"I try to remember the golden rule," Liam said.

"The one who has the gold makes the rules?" she asked, teasing him because she realized she didn't like this part of his world.

"No. Only gamble what you're willing to risk," he said.

She felt the words deep inside. She'd had a similar thought herself when it came to loving this man. And she'd risked it all, and now she was wondering if she was going to be disappointed and angry the way Henry Banner had been. How long was the love bank going to keep floating her money before she had to pay up?

"We're down one player—are the rest of you still in?"
Jameson asked.

"I am," Liam said.

The other two men indicated they were ready to play as
well. Jane backed away but Liam snagged her wrist, holding onto her.

"Stay."

"Um, I don't think that's such a good idea."

She noticed other women at the table, but she wasn't interested in standing behind Liam while he played.

Jane stood on her toes and brushed a kiss against Liam's
chin. "I'm going to watch from over there."

"Ah, baby, stay over here with me," he said, skimming
his hand down her hip.

She flinched as he brushed her tattoo. "What's that?"

"Nothing for you to worry about," she said, walking
away from him. She'd felt lucky and cool earlier, but now
she realized all the luck in the world wasn't going to be
enough to win Liam over.

Screw them. He stalked out of the hotel toward the
garage and got in his car. Today was it. Time for him to stop
dicking around and really do some damage to the Royal
Banner. He wanted that place closed down and then he
wanted to dance in the ashes.

He got as far as his car before he started thinking about
how to make it work. The little fires were frustrating and
hurting business but only incrementally. He needed to do
something big and he needed to do it now.

He wanted to set a blaze that couldn't be controlled or
ignored. The garage smelled of oil and faintly of gasoline.
He'd always liked the smell of gas. He pulled out a pack of
cigarettes and lit one. The ash fluttered to the cement garage
floor.

It'd be hard to get a really good fire going here. Concrete

didn't burn worth a damn. But cars did. All that cloth on the inside and gasoline in the tanks.

He shifted around so he was standing outside the car. No security cameras here. He knew they kept them in the stairwells and the areas around the elevator, but the rest of the garage was one big, blank space. He took the bowie knife out of the duffel bag in the backseat. He'd run out of backpacks after the last fire. Good thing he'd started college so many times.

All those backpacks had added up. Finally put to a good use. But that wasn't important right now. He dropped to the floor and crawled under his car, stubbing out his cigarette before he went any further. He didn't want to burn the shit out of his own face.

He cut two tubes in the undercarriage until he got the gas line. Then he edged out from under the car. He was parked between two other vehicles, so he cut the lines under those two as well. The gasoline bled out in little drips, and he knew if he wanted those cars to really blow he was going to have to be quick about lighting them.

He took his duffel back out of the back of the car and tossed it toward the stairs, then set his lighter to the puddle of gasoline under his car and then the one on the left. The flames moved quickly and he felt that wellspring of panic stirring deep inside him.

He might have started something he couldn't control this time. He lit the gas under the last car and took off, running for the stairs. He grabbed his duffel bag on the way out and heard the first explosion as he hit the stairs. Smoke and flames grew higher as he took the stairs two at a time.

He hid in the shadows at the bottom of the structure. People were spilling out of the hotel, walking over to see what the commotion was about. A couple came down the stairs behind him.

"Are you okay?" the man asked.

"Perfect. You?"

"We're fine. Let's get out of here." The man led the way but he hung back.

He wanted to see who showed up before he went any further.

The game had barely gotten started when Liam's cell phone rang. He glanced down at the caller ID and then back at his cards. The first ones he'd had in a while, and he was going to have to fold. Didi wouldn't be calling unless she'd had a break in the investigation.

"I'm out."

He pushed away from the table. Jane waited for him at the edge of the roped-off area. "What's up?"

"I just needed a break," he said. He didn't want to lie to her but was still reluctant to let her get involved in the arson case. "Let me make a quick call."

He saw the hurt in her eyes before she nodded and walked away from him. God, he was going to have to do some fast talking . . . as soon as this damned investigation was over.

He hit the speed-dial for Didi's number. She answered on the first ring.

"Where are you?"

"In the casino—why?"

"There's a fire at the Royal Banner in the garage. The fire department's on the way."

"Where are you?" Liam asked, making his way through the casino toward the garage area.

"I'm over at the C&H. That homeless guy you interviewed was found dead just a few hours ago across town."

"What the hell—is it related?"

"I haven't had a chance to talk to anyone yet, so who knows, but I'm not going to dismiss it."

"Where's the fire?"

"In the garage area. Can you get out there and case the scene?"

"I'm on my way."

"I am, too. I've got Tod with me."

"This might not be related," Liam said. He stepped outside into the chilly February evening. The smell of smoke was thick in the air as he made his way across the parking lot to the garage. "This is hardly our arsonist's M.O."

"True, but he does seem to hate the Banner Casino Group, and any of their property seems fair game."

There was an explosion as Liam got nearer the four-story garage structure. He stepped back. "Where's the fire department, Didi?"

"Close, why?"

"The cars are starting to go up."

"Damn. Don't go in there."

"Ya think?"

The sound of the fire truck siren was a welcome one. Liam hung up with Didi and ran over to meet the team of first-responders. The fire shouldn't be spreading from one vehicle to another unless the arsonist had left a trail of some kind of accelerant between the cars. If it was even their guy.

"I'm Liam O'Roarke," he said, introducing himself to the crew chief. "Is Danner on duty?"

"No, it's his day off. I'm Deputy-Chief Carlson."

"I'm with the arson investigation team. There was an explosion just before you guys pulled up."

"Thanks for the information. Hang back while we do our job."

Liam stepped back from the fire truck, realizing that for once he wasn't torn about not being able to go in and fight the fire. He saw a crowd gathering from the hotel. Jane stood off to one side, watching him with her eyes narrowed.

She already suspected he had something to do with fire-fighting—why didn't he just come clean and tell her what was really going on?

He started toward her but she shook her head and disappeared into the crowd. He went after her, knowing that whatever she was thinking about him wasn't good.

He couldn't let her go while there was still this tension between them. And he wasn't needed at the scene. He paused for a second, realizing that he wanted to put Jane before the fire. He shook his head. Was this real?

Out of the corner of his eye he noticed someone running away from the garage. He followed the man because witnesses would need to be questioned and not because dealing with the fire situation was home sweet home to him. Unlike the relationship with Jane, which got more complicated by the day.

"Stop!" he yelled.

The man paused and looked over his shoulder. Liam stopped when he recognized him. *Henry Banner.*

Oh, hell. He didn't like the way this looked. Henry entered the hotel through the employee entrance.

Jane came around the corner behind him. "Liam, what are you doing?"

"I can't talk right now," he said.

"Why not? This is ridiculous—I mean, I know that you have a firefighter connection but you can't keep acting like you're—"

"Jane, I can't do this now. I'll explain everything to you later. Go back out front with the rest of the crowd."

She turned on her heel and walked away. Liam entered the building—the hallway was deserted. He didn't waste any time but headed for the elevator that led to the executive offices. He dialed Chase's cell phone number as he moved through the building.

"Banner."

"Liam here. I think Henry's the arsonist."

"What? How can you be sure?"

"He just set another fire—in the garage, and I saw him leaving the scene."

"Did you see him set the fire?" Chase asked.

"No. But he's been around each time the fires have been set."

"So have a lot of other people."

"Listen, I don't want the arsonist to be your brother but everything points to him."

"I'm pulling up to the hotel right now. Where are you?"

"In the elevator going up to your office."

"I'll meet you there and we can finish this discussion."

"Henry saw me follow him into the hotel. I don't know where he is," Liam said.

The elevator doors opened. The receptionist desk was empty.

"Should there be a receptionist at the desk?" Liam asked Chase.

"No. They go off shift at five."

"Is anyone else up here?"

"Yes. Our CFO works late every night until about nine. I can't think of who else would be there. Let me call security. They can check the tape and see where he went."

"I'm going to your office to wait for you."

Chase hung up and Liam pocketed his phone, not content to wait for Chase. He knew Henry had to be here somewhere. He walked down the hall to Chase's office and opened the door.

Chapter 19

Jane knew she should just walk away and do what Liam told her to, but a few minutes later she saw a car pull up and the blonde that Liam spent so much time with climbed out. She was followed by a short, wiry guy with glasses. They went into the building through the employee entrance and Jane followed them.

Once inside the hallway, she followed the sound of their voices to the left. She walked up to them as they were waiting for the elevator.

They said nothing as the car arrived and they all got on board. "Which floor?"

"Umm . . ." She had no idea—she was following them. She should have hung back and waited.

"Which floor?"

"I'm not sure. The executive offices," she said at last. She suspected Liam would be in Chase's office.

"This area is for authorized personnel only," the blonde said.

"I'm a friend of the owner," she said, hoping that Chase would consider their one dinner sufficient for her to claim friendship.

"Yes, but this isn't the time to be in the building here," the man said.

"Chase Banner can tell me that himself," she said.

"Listen—what's your name?"

"Jane."

"I'm Didi and this is Tod. We're here on official fire business and you seriously need to get out of the building."

"Why?" she asked. "I saw another guest came in here."

"Who?" Didi asked.

"Liam."

Tod started to say something but Didi cut him off.

"He's not a guest. He's one of the arson investigators on this case."

She knew he'd been lying to her, but had no idea why. Was it a big secret that he was an arson investigator? "I don't understand any of this."

The elevator car arrived. "Liam will explain it all to you later. But you need to get out of the building right now. The arsonist ran in here and it's going to be dangerous for everyone."

Jane nodded and backed away as the doors closed. She was in over her head with Liam and not in the way she'd thought. Vacation fling, she thought. That's what she'd asked him to be. She had absolutely no right to be upset with him because he didn't confide the details of his life to her.

No matter that her feelings for him had changed and she'd thought . . . God, what an idiot she was to have believed that his feelings had changed. He must just be an affectionate kind of guy. The type of man who lives for the moment and lives each moment fully.

Marcus was like that. He'd tried to explain that he never wanted to miss anything that life had to offer.

But this hurt. She didn't care what his reasons were or that she'd already suspected that he was more than a gambler on vacation. She wanted him to tell her the truth. To trust her. The way she'd trusted him.

She leaned against the wall, bumping her hip where her

new tattoo was, and she realized that she was going to feel a little bit of pain every time she saw it.

She was going to remember Liam O'Roarke and the way he'd reinforced what she'd always known—that men were incapable of being faithful to her.

It didn't matter that Liam wouldn't cheat on her with another woman because he'd already cheated by keeping a big part of his life a secret from her.

"Jane, what are you doing down here?"

Henry was standing at the end of the hallway, looking a little worse for wear. He held a duffel bag loosely in his right hand.

"Nothing. I took a wrong turn and got lost. How do I get back to the casino?"

"I'll show you. I was heading back that way."

She didn't want to bring up the fact that his finances had driven him away from the game, but considering he was a friend, she wanted to make sure he was okay. "Are you going back to the poker game?"

"Ah, no. My house credit ran out."

"That's too bad. I can stake you to a fifty-dollar black-jack game," she said with a smile.

"Thanks, Jane, but I'm not going to be playing in the casinos for a while."

"What are you going to do?" she asked. "Have you decided you've had enough of Vegas?"

"Not exactly," he said, cupping his hand under her elbow and leading her down the hall.

She noticed that he smelled funny, almost like gas. "Where have you been?"

"Trying to find my big brother," Henry said. "Have you seen him?"

"No. But then I was in the poker area until a few minutes ago," she said. Dreaming about being in love and thinking she'd found a man who was . . . something that Liam wasn't. Which he'd warned her about. He'd said he couldn't make promises.

"Did you come outside when the fire started?" Henry asked.

Why was she still in this hallway with Henry? She needed to get moving. Get out of Vegas and back to her regular life. "Yes, did you?"

"Oh, yeah."

She realized that Henry was leading her away from the main hotel area. "I don't think this is the right way. I'm actually really good at navigation and I think—"

"Don't worry about getting lost, Jane. I know where I'm going."

That was the part that worried her. Because she had no idea where they were and her gut instinct said maybe she should have listened to Liam and stayed outside.

Chase got there five minutes after Liam did. Didi and Tod arrived right on his heels. Liam was mad at himself for losing Henry. Where the hell had the little bastard gone?

Chase took a seat in his leather executive's chair. "What the hell is going on? A few days ago we had a list of suspects and tonight you're telling me that our arsonist is my brother."

"I saw him leaving the fire scene," Liam said, not about to defend himself to Chase. His gut had said all along that something was going on with Henry.

"You thought he was using drugs again—you'll be surprised to learn that he checked in this morning and passed his monthly drug test."

"I'm happy to hear that. I think the weird behavior stemmed from the fires he was starting," Liam said.

"That is one of the things consistent in the behavior of arsonists," Didi added. "We see it all the time."

"Maybe you do," Chase said. "But my brother is just having a hard time adjusting to being sober and trying to make his life work. I think you're turning to him because he's a convenient scapegoat."

Liam ran his hands through his hair, totally frustrated. "Do you think I want to be standing here telling you your brother is the man who's been starting all these fires?"

Tod stepped forward. "Our investigation points to Henry Banner. We have found a paper trail of credit card receipts that show Henry purchased the accelerants used in the string of fires."

"Who are you?" Chase asked.

He was at his most condescending whenever something concerned Henry. Liam was afraid that Chase might say something that would get him thrown in jail. He'd always been so protective of his little brother.

"Tod Courtney, ATF," Tod said, holding out his hand.

Chase ignored the hand and turned on Liam. "Since when is the ATF involved in this?"

"Since more than a million dollars in damage has occurred," Tod said. "That kind of damage isn't something the government can just ignore, especially with the escalation of fires. This is a highly populated area."

"Why wasn't I informed?" Chase demanded, pushing to his feet.

Liam shook his head. "We don't have time for this. We need to find Henry. He came into the hotel and I thought I was following him up here, but now I don't know where he is. We need to find him before he starts another fire."

"Fine," Chase said. He hit a button on a remote on his desk and the side panels on one of the walls rolled back to reveal several monitors, all in black-and-white. All of them showed different areas of the casino.

"I don't know what he looks like so I won't be any help,"

Tod said, moving back to the side of the room. "Do you have a photo we can circulate?"

"Yes," Chase said.

Didi and Liam stayed in front of the wall of monitors. Liam kept his gaze fixed on the monitors, scanning the different areas, searching for something. Some break.

"I saw your Jane downstairs," Didi said, never taking her eyes off the monitors.

"Where?" Liam asked, forcing himself to keep his concentration on the monitors when he really wanted to turn to Didi and find out every detail of her conversation with Jane.

"In the hallway—she tried to come up here with Tod and me. We sent her back outside. She didn't know you were on the investigation, did she?"

Liam rubbed the back of his neck. "I was undercover."

"Yeah, I think you're going to have to explain that to her. She looked . . . I don't know. Angry, and a little sad."

Liam cursed under his breath. He hadn't handled the situation with her very well.

Didi reached over and touched his forearm. "Don't think about her right now. We need to find our arsonist before he hits again. And if he knows you saw him, he's going to be even more determined to do more damage before we catch him."

"I know that. I've been a firefighter all my life, Didi. Nothing is more important to me than fire." He wished his words were true but he was his father's son—Derrick O'Roarke would have cut off his own hand before allowing anyone else to see his emotions. So Liam sucked up his own feelings at the thought of hurting Jane and focused on the one thing he did best.

The screens moved every fifteen seconds to the next quadrant in their rotation. Without knowing exactly where Henry was in the building, or if he was even still in the building, it was like looking for a needle in a haystack.

Tod and Chase were working on the computer—he and Didi kept scanning the screens.

"Where would he go?" Liam asked under his breath.

"A guest room would be my hunch. He's started almost every fire from a guest room."

"Agreed. But he'd need a key."

"The security tape from the last fire shows him behind the front desk," Didi said. "Chase, how do we get the cameras from the front desk up?"

"And we'll also need the guest hallways," Liam added.

Henry came over to them with a remote in his hand. He pushed a few buttons and they saw the screen switch to the reception area of the lobby. The front desk was busy and Chase froze the screen so they could all study it.

"I don't see him. What about behind the desk? Can you pull up that angle?" Liam asked.

Chase hit a few more buttons but they couldn't identify Henry in any of the frames. "Maybe he's already been there. Someone needs to go down to security and review the last ten minutes of tape from the front desk."

"I'll go," Tod said.

Tod left and Chase hit another button to change the other monitors to the guest hallways. Flames and smoke filled the hallway. Liam leaned closer to the screen as a couple walked toward a room. Jane's room. "He's with Jane."

Liam felt a rising sense of panic as he ran toward Jane's room, though a part of him knew that arson and murder were two different types of crime and most arsonists, especially ones like Henry, seldom killed to start fires.

There's always a first time, he thought. He wasn't surprised to hear the fire alarm go off as he broke out into the casino. There was no way to get to the guest tower from the executive offices except through the freakin' casino.

Everyone was a little panicked, some running and some just not sure where to go or what to do. He forced himself toward the wall and around most of the people milling about in the lobby. When he was finally free of the crowd he broke into a run again.

He was intimately familiar with the emergency stairwell and took the stairs two at a time. His mind filled with images of all the things that could happen to Jane. Why hadn't he made sure she'd gone back to the front of the hotel?

When he got to the thirty-fifth floor he realized he was going to have to use a pickax to get through it. He didn't have the key to open the door from this side. Hell, where was his head?

Even a probie knew better than to go off half-cocked in a dangerous situation. He turned back to the fire case, knowing there'd be an ax in there, but heard the sound of footsteps in the stairwell.

"I've got the key," Chase said. Didi was right on his heels, along with two firefighters in turn-out gear.

"We go in first," a fireman said.

Liam stood back, knowing they were right. Fires were nothing to mess with but all he could see in his mind was Jane. And he wanted—no, needed—to get to her.

The fire wasn't his first priority and he was glad for it. He knew he could get in there and save her.

Chase used his passkey to open the door as huge waves of billowing smoke filled the stairwell. They all dropped low to breathe in the clear air.

"Stay here," one of the firemen said.

They both entered the hallway and he glanced at Chase and Didi. They weren't trained, so they should both stay. "I'll be back."

"Liam—"

"I can't stay. I've trained my entire life to go into burning buildings, and now Jane is trapped in there. I can't wait."

Didi nodded and handed him an oxygen mask. "I got this from one of the guys downstairs. Be careful."

He put on the mask, stepping toward the hallway. Chase stopped him with a hand on his arm. "Try to get Henry out if you can."

Liam nodded.

He entered the hallway, feeling the heat gathering around them. This blaze was bigger than the last two. He doubted there'd be anything left of Jane's room, but he had to start there. The sprinklers were working, soaking everything, but still the blaze burned.

The firefighters had forced open all the doors as they went down the hallway, and Liam knew they would have made a clean sweep of each room and ascertained they were empty.

He kept moving, trying not to envision Jane passed out from smoke inhalation, but it was damned hard not to picture the worst because he'd seen it.

He followed the fire hose and found the firemen dousing the blaze in Jane's room. He signaled that he'd continue clearing the floor while they fought the blaze. He knew he had to keep focused on the fire, not on Jane.

He picked up the ax one of them had dropped and went to the next room. A quick touch of the door told him that the blaze continued in that room. The next door wasn't hot, and there was no smoke escaping under the door.

He lifted the ax, slicing through the door in two powerful downward chops. He kicked the remains of the door out of the way and stepped inside.

He almost tripped over Jane. He was so happy to see her he felt tears sting his eyes. She was slumped over on the floor. He saw a bruise and blood dripping down the side of her face. He felt around for her pulse and found it weak and thready but there.

He lifted her to the bed and set her there while he went into the bathroom to get a towel to tie over her mouth and nose. She couldn't afford to inhale any more smoke.

He tied the towel around the bottom half of her face, then he picked her up and tossed her over his shoulder. He went out into the hallway where the firefighters were still battling the blaze. More men from their crew had come to help back them up.

Liam showed them where he'd stopped clearing the rooms and went down the hall quickly. When he stepped out into the hall, Didi was the only one standing there.

"She needs an EMT. Can you take her downstairs?"

Didi took Jane's body, putting her over her shoulder the same way Liam had. "Chase wouldn't stay put. He's gone to the emergency stairwell on the other side of the building to see if Henry will come out that way."

"I'm going back in to help finish clearing the floor," Liam said.

"I called the cops and we've got them posted at all exits to the building. Tod distributed the photo of Henry, so there's no way he's going to make it out of the building."

"Let's hope that doesn't make him do something stupid."

"Agreed. Be careful, big guy. Even you aren't invincible."

But he always had been in a fire. "Fire I can handle."

He turned away from the women and reentered the smoke-filled hallway, knowing that somewhere in there was the arsonist and that he was going to be the one to find him.

Chapter 20

Henry didn't know exactly when his plan for the fire had gotten out of his control. Jane had been a complication he hadn't anticipated but he'd handled her easily enough. She hadn't really wanted to agitate him. She'd actually said that.

Like he was some kind of psycho she had to placate. Well, he'd placated that bitch into silence and left her in a room that should be filled with smoke by now. The fire-fighters were loud with their axes and hoses, and he was careful to stay just a few steps ahead of them.

But he knew this time he was going to have a hard time escaping. Not just the hotel, but Vegas. That scared him be-cause he knew he couldn't survive outside of this world. As fucked-up as it was, he really only knew how to live here. Only knew how to survive here.

The fires . . . they were a bit of fun, a way to tweak Chase and get his eagle-eyed attention off of him for a while, but now . . . now it looked like even the fire was moving out of his control.

He finally made it to the other end of the hallway. The smoke was making its way toward him, the fire drawing all the oxygen it could. He pushed open the door.

Everyone thought they were so smart, having figured out who he was, but he was having the last laugh. There was no way they could catch him.

He was invincible. He took the stairs two at a time, skidding to a halt when he saw Chase coming up.

"Henry, thank God you're okay," Chase said. There was a note of real concern in his voice. He knew his brother loved him. Chase had always looked out for him. Or at least used to, before he married Wendy. Then he'd become so critical of everything he did. Made him go to rehab.

"Chase . . ."

"Don't say anything. I've got my lawyer downstairs and we're going to figure this out."

Henry shook his head. Chase couldn't bail him out again. This was his way of getting back at Chase, and his brother had to know that. "I don't think so. Not this time."

"But you've made a clean start. You know it and I know it. We'll explain this away. Some kind of PTSD left over from all those years of using."

"No," Henry said. "The only problem is you, big brother."

"Problem?" Chase asked. "I've spent my entire life getting you out of trouble or covering for you. Don't say I'm the one who's ruined your life."

"That's just it, Chase. You're so damned perfect all the time. But not this time. You can't control the fire and I can."

"Henry, you're not controlling anything. The firefighters are putting out the blaze up there. Is that what this is about? Control?"

Henry shrugged. "It's about me winning."

"How do you figure?"

"You tricked me out of my share of the Banner Casino Group and now I'm getting even. You've lost a lot of profit the last few weeks and that's all my doing, big brother."

"I didn't trick you out of your shares—you wanted to cash out to buy drugs, remember? I bought you out."

"Of course you have to bring the drugs into it. It's never been good enough for you that I'm clean and sober now, is it?"

"Of course that's enough for me. The fact that you've taken up fire-starting isn't exactly proof that you're dealing with your life."

"I told you why I did it. To make you pay."

Chase shook his head. He looked a lot like their father used to look right before he gave a lecture.

Henry took another step closer to his brother. He could tell Chase didn't know what to do now. "I'm leaving. I'm not talking to your lawyer or doing any of the things you have planned for me."

"Henry, you can't leave. There are cops at all the exits."

Anger sparked inside him, fierce and out of control. He lashed out, hitting Chase in the jaw and knocking him backward down the stairs. He fell down the short flight, then lay at the bottom.

"Fuck. Chase?"

He ran down the stairs. The angle of his brother's head wasn't good. Dammit, why had Chase made him lose his temper? He felt around under Chase's head, pulling his hand back when he felt the dampness.

Blood soaked his hand and he wiped it on his pants and pushed himself away. Dammit, he'd killed his brother. What the fuck was he going to do now?

How the hell was he going to get out of this? He cradled his brother's body in his arms, stroking Chase's head.

He felt around for a pulse and found one. It was weak and he wished he knew what to do. But he had no clue. He did know how to control fire but somehow he didn't know how to help Chase now.

"What happened, Henry?"

Henry glanced up at Liam O'Roarke, standing on the stairs above them. Henry got to his feet and backed away. Liam would take care of Chase.

"He fell."

Liam came further down the stairs, an oxygen mask in one hand. He set the mask on the stairs and bent over Chase.

He had this one moment, this one choice; he could help Liam with his brother or he could make a break and run for it. Chances were, either way he was going to jail. He looked down at Chase and thought about how things never really worked out the way he planned them. But he knew he couldn't let his brother die.

"He needs help," he said.

"I'm going to call 911," Liam said.

Jane woke up in the back of the EMT truck. Her head ached and she felt her heart beating in her temple. She wished that her memory was foggy but she remembered every detail of how she'd ended up here.

She'd tried to talk to Henry, but she'd been a little impatient and obviously that had angered him.

"Oh my God, are you okay?"

"Yes, Shanna. Thanks for coming. I didn't know who else to call."

"Good thing you called me. I'll take care of you."

"I really need my BlackBerry so I can text Josef and let him know that my parents are coming to get me."

"I can do that. Mitchell was with me when I got your call. I'll have him handle Josef."

"Thanks, Shanna."

"Oh, honey, you don't look so good."

"I have a concussion."

"I know. Where are you meeting your folks?"

"Here. They are coming to the hotel. I didn't know where else to tell them to meet me." She was rambling but couldn't seem to stop the words. She really wasn't cut out for emergencies. This was her second one, and if she never experienced another one, that'd be okay with her.

Shanna brushed her hair back from her face and tugged the blanket the EMTs had given her higher on her shoulders. Jane was soaking wet from the sprinklers and chilled to the bone. She wanted to get out of Vegas and couldn't wait for her parents to get here.

She needed them. She thought maybe she even needed Dick Clark's *Rockin' New Year's Eve*. Because that was who she was inside. Changing wasn't working for her. She felt worse now than she ever had during her entire marriage and subsequent divorce.

"I heard the cops say that they caught the arsonist. He confessed to everything."

"That's good. He made it out alive?" Jane asked. She had some lingering anger toward Henry for hitting her, but she figured he had bigger issues now. The EMTs had told her that a firefighter had rescued her.

That had been enough. She was so tired.

"Let me talk to the EMT in charge and find out what I need to do and then we'll get you out of here," Shanna said.

She watched her friend walk away, leaning back against the side of the truck. Smoke still poured from the side of the hotel but the flames were under control. The cop cars were pulling away and in the distance she saw a tall figure. Liam was moving easily amongst the firefighters and other authorities, talking to them all and doing his thing.

She didn't blame him for his secrecy—not anymore. But it still hurt because she'd given him so many opportunities to tell her the truth, to tell her about his life away from Vegas, and he never had.

She felt a wave of melancholy wash over her and hoped it was from the bump on the head. She'd never been easily depressed, but it was hard for her to find the silver lining in everything that had happened between her and Liam.

Hard to see the bright side.

232 / *Katherine Garbera*

"Okay, Jane. Let's go. You can shower and get changed and even sleep, but I have to wake you up every few hours and make sure you're responsive."

"Do you mind?" Shanna had a full schedule.

"You're the best friend I have—I want to keep you around and in good shape."

"Thanks," Jane said, hugging Shanna with one arm.

"I've never been so scared in my entire life."

"Me, either. When the EMTs called me and said you were here . . . I'm just glad you're okay."

They worked their way through the crowd toward the front of the hotel. Wendy Banner was coming out as they were walking in.

"Oh, Jane. Are you okay? I just heard most of the details."

"I'm fine. How's everyone else?"

"Henry's in custody. And Chase has a bad concussion. They're taking him to the hospital for observation."

"Will he be okay?"

"I hope so."

"Please let me know when you hear something definitive," Jane said.

Wendy nodded. "I will."

She dashed out toward a waiting Town Car. When they got to the lobby, Wendy went to check on the status of her room. Everything in Jane's had been destroyed.

"Ms. Monte? I'm Officer Franklin—I need to get a statement from you."

She gave the officer her description of what had happened. Reliving it made her head ache and made her feel so tired and small. Eventually he had it all down on his form and then reread it to her and asked her to sign it.

She did and then leaned back against the padded headrest of the chair she was sitting in and closed her eyes.

This day had been the most tumultuous of her life. She'd

wanted excitement when she'd come to Vegas, but this was too much.

"Jane?"

She opened her eyes to see Shanna standing there. "You ready to go up?"

"Yes. I'm going to need some clean clothes."

"What size?"

"Six."

"I'll get Mitchell on it."

"I'm sure he'll love that."

"He's worried about you, too," Shanna said, putting her arm around Jane and leading her to the elevator. It was nice to have the support of her friends, but the one person she really longed for was Liam.

And other than that one brief glance she'd had while they were outside, she hadn't seen him. And she had the feeling that she wouldn't see him again. Their vacation fling was definitely over now that his investigation had been concluded.

The paperwork and the interviews took forever. Liam had tried to break away several times but there was always one more person who needed an answer.

"I can handle this from here," Didi said. "We're going to need an official statement from Chase about what happened in the stairwell. Do you want to go get it?"

Hell, no, but Liam knew that it was part of his job. And he did want to check on his friend.

"Yeah, I'll go. Do you need me for anything else here?"

"Not now. I'll page you if I need you."

"Make sure it's before midnight."

"Planning on turning into a pumpkin?"

"No, but I will be out of touch if I have my way," Liam said. He knew he had his work cut out for him with Jane, but now that he'd wrapped up the investigation he could concentrate on her.

He took a cab to the hospital, where he was directed to the ER cubicle where Chase was. He was propped up in the bed with Wendy hovering over him.

"Liam, thanks for saving him," Wendy said. She came over to him and gave him a quick hug.

"It was nothing. Henry was already doing his part when I got there."

"I'm sure. After he almost killed Chase, he tried to save him," Wendy said. Sarcasm really didn't suit her.

"I have to take Chase's statement. Do you want to go get a drink or something while I do that?" Liam asked.

"Is that your nice way of asking me to leave?" she countered.

"Yes."

"Okay, I'll be back in fifteen." She bent down and gave Chase a kiss on the forehead and then left.

"She's pretty protective of you."

"Don't I know it. Do you really need a statement from me?" Chase asked. His eyes were dilated and he kept squinting.

"Is the light too much for you?" Liam asked, because he knew that light sensitivity was sometimes a side effect of concussions.

"Nah, I'm fine. What happened to Henry?" Chase asked, his concern for his brother evident in his voice.

"He helped me with you, calling 911 and all that. Then the police took him into custody. Jasmine Crotty, your lawyer, was there with him the entire time. He's not going to get off scot-free but she's already working on the case."

"I'll call her later," Chase said. Liam felt sorry for his friend because he knew that this incident was far from over for the Banner family.

Liam would be able to leave Vegas and finish up his paperwork, maybe come back and testify at a trial, but he could move on. He didn't have to live with the knowledge that someone in his family had tried to burn down his business.

"Much later. You need time to recover. Why the hell didn't you stay put like I told you to."

Chase sighed and shrugged his left shoulder. "He's my kid brother. I couldn't let you or some other guy confront him. I knew if I could just talk to him . . ."

"Talking didn't get the job done, did it?" Liam asked, because Henry hadn't been in the mood to listen to anyone. Even when he'd come down those stairs, he hadn't known how Henry would react.

"No, it didn't."

Liam doubted that Chase would ever tell him what had happened in the stairwell. But as he sat next to his friend, writing out his statement, he realized that Chase had changed in just those few hours.

"It's not your fault," Liam said, guessing where Chase was going in his head.

"I don't know about that. He said that everything was easy for me."

Liam didn't believe that. "You've worked damned hard for everything you have."

"Yeah, but Dad did cut me a break when I was younger. Took me to work a lot more often then he took Henry. Dad and I were much closer."

Liam didn't buy it. "I've got three younger siblings and they are all capable of standing on their own."

Chase rubbed his forehead. "That's another thing Henry said. That I was always fixing things for him. Do you think I should have let him go to jail?"

Chase didn't really expect an answer, but Liam thought of his baby sister Andi and how she'd had to move away to find her own path in life. "Jail wouldn't have fixed Henry. He's too soft for that. But maybe being on his own, out of your town and your shadow . . . who knows? He probably would have struggled anyway."

Liam finished writing up the report and handed it to Chase to sign.

"How's Jane? I heard she'd been hurt."

"I don't know. I haven't had a chance to see her yet. I think I lost ten years off my life when I found her huddled in that room, unconscious."

Chase closed his eyes. "Please tell her how sorry I am that she got in the middle of this."

"The blame belongs with me. I'm the one who didn't make sure she was safely out of harm's way. I knew Henry was inside the building and instead of making sure she was safe . . ."

"Henry's the one who hurt her, Liam. Not you and not I. We both have to remember we're not responsible for his actions."

Chase's words made sense and Liam knew that, but another part of him also knew he had to live with the consequences of his own actions. He hadn't taken any more time with Jane because he hadn't wanted to answer her questions about what he was doing.

"After I file the report on this, I'm going to be on vacation, but if you need anything, call my cell."

Chase nodded.

"Where you going?"

"I don't know yet. That all depends on Jane."

Wendy came back and once he was sure they were okay, he left the hospital. He didn't really know what he was going to say to Jane, but tonight he'd learned the real truth. He didn't want to live without her.

Chapter 21

The knock on Shanna's door just before midnight had both of them looking at each other. Her parents had called and they were still a few hours away.

"Who is it?"

"Liam O'Roarke. I'm a friend of Jane's."

Shanna looked at her. "The blond guy?"

Jane nodded.

"Should I let him in?"

"Yes," Jane said. She couldn't exactly hide from him. Besides, closure was good. That was the one thing she'd never had with Rodney, since he'd snuck off in the middle of the night like the dirty little rat he was.

Shanna opened the door and then stepped back to let Liam in. He hadn't changed clothes since the fire. His shirt was stained and charred and stuck to his skin. His hair was matted on one side and sticking out on the other.

He looked a mess but she was so glad to see him.

"Can I talk to you alone?" Liam asked Jane.

"Um . . . this is Shanna's room."

Shanna stood up. "Give me a minute to get dressed and then I'm out of your hair. She can't be alone because of the concussion, so call me before you leave."

Shanna changed in record time and was out the door. Jane snuggled down deeper into the pillows, hating that she felt so small and puny. Liam came further into the room as soon as Shanna left. He sat down on her side of the bed.

"I don't know where to start."

"With what? The truth?" she asked.

He nodded.

"I think the best thing is just to say it."

She wasn't sure what to expect. She knew from what he'd said earlier that he wasn't going to be sticking around. But why would he come here?

"I came to Vegas because Chase asked me to after the first fire. I . . . I work for a private arson investigation firm, Hot Heads."

"That's nice."

"Jane . . ." he said in a warning tone.

"I'm sorry, but I feel like this is too little, too late. I figured it all out. You needed me as part of your cover, didn't you?"

Liam pushed to his feet and paced away from her, pushing the drapes aside and staring out at the lights of the Vegas Strip. She was tired of that sight and couldn't wait to put it behind her.

"I did use you as part of my cover, but—"

"No buts. I know you set me up with Wendy so I could dig up more information on Henry. What a boon for you that I ran into him that night in the casino."

He turned back around, facing her. "Are you going to forgive me for this?"

She shrugged. "I don't know."

"This is about more than one omission, isn't it?"

"I thought you were different," she said. "I thought you were the kind of guy who I could trust to be honest with me."

"I am that kind of man. Jane, baby, believe me when I say that I wanted to tell you."

"God, don't say that. I can't tell you how many times I heard that from my ex when I confronted him with some lie or other."

He shook his head. "I'm not your ex and I've never lied to you. The investigation wasn't mine to let out of the bag. No matter how much I knew I could trust you, I needed to keep all the balls in the air the way I did."

She understood that, she really did. "It's not you."

"What?"

"I'm mad at myself because I wanted to believe you were this carefree, bad-boy gambler who wanted nothing else in life but to win a high-stakes game. I wanted to believe that I was your lucky charm."

Liam came and sat back down beside her. "You are my lucky charm. For a long time I've been adrift. Firefighting was all I ever knew, and when that wasn't enough for me anymore, I was lost.

"But ever since you came into my life . . . it's like I've found something that was missing. I'm almost forty years old and I've just realized that you're what I need to make my life complete."

"We hardly know each other," she said, but she felt the sincerity in his words all the way to her soul.

"I love you, Jane. I've never said that to another woman."

She looked up at him and knew deep inside that she loved him, too, but she was afraid to say the words.

"Trust me, baby," he said.

"I love you, too. But you only wanted a vacation fling."

He drew her gently into his arms. "I want so much more than a few naughty memories. I want a lifetime with you."

She snuggled close to him. "I can't get married to you right away. I did that once and it was a big mistake."

"As long as you're by my side, that's all I need."

* * *

Jane Monte saw her life flash before her eyes as she walked down the beach toward Liam O'Roarke. Waves from the Atlantic ocean rolled on the shore, filling the air with the scent of the sea. She couldn't believe how much her life had changed since that fire in the Royal Banner hotel. Looking at Liam in his white Hawaiian-print shirt and khaki surf shorts, she couldn't be happier.

She was wearing not a revealing negligee, but a white wraparound dress. She had a white lily tucked over one ear and Shanna had flown to Florida to act as her maid of honor.

Her parents and brother were standing in a small group with Liam's family. The O'Roarkes were loud but a lot of fun. They'd made her feel welcome over the last year while she and Liam had dated. They'd contemplated a wedding in Vegas, but in the end they wanted to get married in a place where they'd be spending the rest of their lives.

Wendy and Chase Banner were standing next to Jane's parents, their little girls acting as flower girls for the ceremony. Instead of scattering flower petals, they had made a path of sea shells earlier in the day to mark where Jane should walk.

Now, as Liam's nephew played the "Wedding March" on his guitar, she walked toward him. His eyes were black as night and very calm. *Very serious.* She'd had a few doubts about committing herself to marriage again, but it was hard to panic when faced with his utter confidence.

When she got to his side, he pulled her close and kissed her deeply before the officiate could start the ceremony. There were a few hoots and hollers from the O'Roarkes.

When the ceremony was over, Liam lifted her up in his arms and showed her off to his family. "My lucky charm."

She smiled to herself thinking that she was the lucky one. Lucky to have found a bad boy who was the very best man for her.

*   *   *

Later that evening Liam carried her over the threshold of his small oceanfront house. Liam made a beeline for the bedroom.

He put her on her feet next to the bed. "I can't believe you're really here, Mrs. O'Roarke."

"Me either," she said. Truly she was afraid to believe in the happiness that swamped her.

He leaned down and kissed her so tenderly before slowly undressing her. When she was standing naked in front of him, he traced the shamrock tattoo at her hip.

"Why?"

She felt more vulnerable now than she had just a second before. "I didn't want to forget you. I wanted a reminder of reclaiming myself and my femininity."

"So you took my tattoo?" he asked, bending down to trace the design with his tongue.

"Yes, I did."

She couldn't think as he stood back up and lifted her onto the bed. He bent down to capture the tip of her breast in his mouth. He sucked her deep in his mouth, his teeth lightly scraping against her sensitive flesh. His other hand played at her other breast arousing her, making her arch against him in need.

She reached between them and took his erection in her hand, bringing him closer to her. Spreading her legs wider so that she was totally open to him. "I need you now."

He lifted his head; the tips of her breasts were damp from his mouth and very tight. He rubbed his chest over them, before sliding deep into her body.

She slid her hands down his back, cupping his butt as he thrust deeper into her. Their eyes met; staring deep into his eyes made her feel like their souls were meeting. She felt her body start to tighten around him catching her by surprise. She climaxed before him. He gripped her hips, holding her down and thrusting into her two more times before he came with a loud grunt of her name.

She slid her hands up his back and kissed him deeply. "You are so much better than a tattoo."

His deep laughter washed over her and she felt like she'd found her place here. Not old Jane or new Jane, but Jane O'Roarke.

Try Karen Kelley's
DOUBLE DATING WITH THE DEAD,
available now from Brava . . .

"Boo," a woman said in a very dry, sultry voice from behind him.

He whirled around. For a split second he thought the place might actually be haunted. But if he was seeing a ghost, he hoped she didn't vanish anytime soon. She looked pretty damned sweet as she stood in the open doorway.

No, not sweet. Nothing about her looked sweet. She was earth, wind and fire all rolled up into one magnificent woman. The combination was sexy as hell.

Slowly his gaze traveled over her, past long black hair that draped over one shoulder to kiss a breast. She was like nothing he'd ever seen with her loose white shirt, bangles at her wrists and a multicolored full skirt.

Selena James looked even better in color than she had in the grainy black-and-white photo above her weekly psychic column in the newspaper.

He wondered if she knew that with the sunlight streaming in behind her, the skirt she wore was practically transparent. He didn't think he wanted to tell her. He rather enjoyed the view. Payback for the very public challenge she'd issued in the paper just because he'd said she was delusional—on television.

A twinge of guilt flickered over him. He quickly dismissed

it. The woman *was* delusional. There were no such things as ghosts or people who talked to ghosts.

"Did I scare you?" she asked in a mocking voice, one eyebrow lifting sardonically. She swept into the room, and shadows blocked the view of her legs.

A shame because he could've looked at Selena James's legs a lot longer.

"I don't scare so easily." He casually leaned against the balustrade and crossed his arms in front of him.

"But then you've never stayed in a haunted hotel," she said.

"I can't stay in a place that's haunted since there are no such things as ghosts."

As she stepped closer, he could see her eyes were a deep, haunting violet, her features pure, patrician. And she was tall. Maybe five-eight. For some reason he'd pictured her much shorter.

When she breezed past him, he caught the scent of her perfume. It wrapped around him, begging him to follow wherever she might lead. She was definitely a temptation, but one he'd resist. After all, she was the enemy.

She faced him, and his heart skipped a beat. Knowing she was the enemy didn't make her any less alluring and sexy. Probably the reason she had so many followers who faithfully read her column. She was like a spider, weaving her web for the unsuspecting fly. But he knew her game and wouldn't be drawn in. No, Miss James had finally met her match.

Definitely tempting, though.

Man, he'd been spending way too many hours closeted away in front of his computer while he met his last deadline, then been consumed with promotion for his current release, *Ghosts and Other Guff.* Dating hadn't been a top priority.

Two weeks alone with Selena might not be so bad. She was hot, definitely hot. He wondered how hard it would be to entice her into his bed. At least then his stay here wouldn't be such a waste. It was an option worth considering.

Selena watched Trent. The changing emotions on his face that finally settled into speculation.

Would she or wouldn't she?

She'd seen that interested look before in men's eyes. Trent wasn't bad himself—even better in person than he had been on television, which was what started this whole mess. Sure, it was only a local station, but he'd said she was obviously delusional. Announced it on television without a care in the world.

So if he thought she'd be climbing in his bed, he'd better think again.

She didn't care that his shoulders were wide and his eyes a bright green, the color of finely cut emeralds. The kind of eyes, and the kind of smile, that could talk her right out of her clothes and have her naked on a bed before she realized how she'd gotten there.

Oh, yes, he was a clean-shaven devil in an expensive suit and, if she wasn't mistaken, wearing designer cologne.

But she wasn't stupid and she wouldn't fall for his charm. He'd figure that out soon enough.

Trent was a skeptic. Her enemy. He'd made jokes about her column. She could very well lose her job if she didn't change his opinion about the supernatural by the end of their stay.

Lust could not enter the equation.

She faced him once again, tilting her chin and looking up at him. He was very tall, too. "You said some pretty ugly things about me on television. Do you always take potshots at people you've never met?"

"Nothing personal."

Was he serious? The bangles on her wrists jangled when

she planted her hands on her hips. "Nothing personal? You're joking, right?"

She gritted her teeth. She would *not* stoop to losing her temper. But she'd love to wipe that sardonic smirk right off his face!

His smile turned downward, and it was like a thunder-cloud hovered over him. Well, she was the lightning bolt that would strike him down.

"I go after all cheats, not just you," he said.

"Now I'm a cheat?" *I won't lose my temper*, she told her-self.

"You're bilking the public when you feed them a line of crap about ghosts being everywhere and that you can talk to them."

"And how do you know they aren't?"

He swung his arm wide. "Do you see any?" He looked toward the second floor. "If there are any ghosts here, show yourselves," he yelled.

Silence.

He looked at her. "See, no ghosts."

If there were any in the old hotel, he'd probably pissed them off. One thing she hated more than a skeptic was a pissed-off ghost. They could get really nasty when they were riled.

"I wouldn't do that if I were you," she warned.

Christmas just got a whole lot hotter in
I'M YOUR SANTA,
coming next month from Brava.
Here's an excerpt from
Lori Foster's "The Christmas Present,"
the first story in this sexy anthology . . .

With each step he took, Levi pondered what to say to Beth. She needed to understand that she'd disappointed him.

Infuriated him.

Befuddled him and inflamed him.

In order to get a handle on things, he had to get a handle on her. He had to convince Beth to admit to her feelings.

He needed time and space to accomplish that.

Thanks to Ben's directions, Levi carried her through the kitchen toward the back storage unit, where interruptions were less likely to occur.

The moment he reached the dark, private area, Levi paused. Time to give Beth a piece of his mind. Time to be firm, to insist that she stop denying the truth.

Time to set her straight.

But then he looked at her—and he forgot about his important intentions. He forgot everything because of his need for this one particular woman.

God, she took him apart without even trying.

Among the shelves of pots and pans, canned goods and bags of foodstuff, Levi slowly lowered Beth to her feet.

He couldn't seem to do more than stare at her.

Worse, she stared back, all big dark eyes, damp lips, and barely banked desire. Denial might come from her mouth, but the truth was there in her expression.

When she let out a shuddering little breath, Levi lost the battle, the war . . . he lost his heart all over again.

Crushing her close, he freed all the restraints he'd imposed while she was his best friend's fiancée. He gave free rein to his need to consume her. Physically. Emotionally. Forever and always.

Moving his hands over her, absorbing the feel of her, he tucked her closer still and took her mouth. How could he have forgotten how perfectly she tasted? How delicious she smelled and how indescribable it felt to hold her?

Even after their long weekend together, he hadn't been sated. He'd never be sated.

Levi knew if he lived to be a hundred and ten, he'd still be madly in love with Beth Monroe.

The fates had done him in the moment he'd first met her. She smiled and his world lit up. She laughed and he felt like Zeus, mythical and powerful. She talked about marrying Brandon and the pain was more than anything he'd ever experienced in his twenty-nine years.

Helpless, that's what he'd been.

So helpless that it ate at him day and night.

Then, by being unfaithful, Brandon had proved that he didn't really love Beth after all—and all bets were off.

When Beth came to him that night, hurt and angry, and looking to him for help, Levi threw caution to the wind and gave her all she requested, and all she didn't know to ask for.

He gave her everything he could, and prayed she'd recognize it for the deep unshakable love he offered, not just a sexual fling meant for retaliation.

But . . . she hadn't.

She'd been too shaken by her own free response, a response she gave every time he touched her.

A response she gave right now.

They thumped into the wall, and Levi recovered from his tortured memories, brought back to the here and now.

He had Beth.

She wanted him.

Until she grasped the enormity of their connection, he'd continue pursuing her.

Lured by the sensuality of the moment, Levi levered himself against her, and loved it. As busy as his hands might be, Beth's were more so. Small, cool palms coasted over his nape, into his hair, then down to his shoulders. Burning him through the layers of his flannel shirt and tee, her touch taunted him and spurred his lust.

Wanting her, right here and right now, Levi pressed his erection against her belly and then cradled her body as she shuddered in reaction, doing her best to crawl into him.

His mouth against hers, he whispered, "I need you, Beth."

Beyond any real verbal response, Beth moaned and clutched at him.

And that gave him pause, because Levi knew she was with him—and he knew that she'd hate herself for it later.

Damn it.

Don't miss Shelly Laurenston's
THE MANE EVENT,
coming next month from Brava . . .

Dez woke up cursing. The ring of her damn cell phone completely disrupted her lovely dream involving Mace, her, and her handcuffs.

She grabbed for the phone on her nightstand. Knocked it off. Reached down and grabbed for it. Fell out of bed. Hit one of the dogs in the process. Wrestled the phone from the dog's mouth. Then groggily crawled on all fours back into her warm and cozy bed.

"MacDermot," Dez mumbled into the phone, assuming it would be work.

"Hey."

Dez's arms went out from under her when that voice tore through her dazed, sleep-drowned mind and she landed flat on her face. Mace and that voice of his slid all the way down to her clit and moved in.

Why the hell was he calling her? What the hell was his deal? And how the hell did he get her number anyway? All right. Forget that last stupid question. He probably had a full background check done on her by now. The man was a SEAL after all.

Not knowing what else to say, Dez hit him with the first thing that came to mind. "Who is this?"

She crossed her eyes. Well those brilliant phrases kept rolling right from her mouth. *You're such an idiot, MacDermot.*

258 / *Shelly Laurenston*

"It's Mace."

"Oh," she replied casually like she didn't almost come from his "hey" alone. "Hiya, Mace." She used her shoulder to cover the mouthpiece on her phone, shoved a pillow over her face, and yelled into it. After a moment, she calmly went back to the conversation. "What's up?"

She heard him stretch. "Nothing. Just checking on you."

She closed her eyes and her legs. Took a calming breath. "Oh. That's sweet."

"I'm known for being sweet."

"No, you're not."

He laughed softly and she bit her lip to keep from moaning.

Really . . . is there anything better than the gravelly six A.M. voice on a man? Dez didn't think so. And Mace had one of those in spades. She may have to dig out her vibrator. *It has to be around here somewhere.*

"You're right. I'm not." A moment of silence descended and Dez wondered if they already ran out of things to say. She should have known better.

"You just getting up?"

"Not really. It's only six A.M. and I don't have to go to work. So, I'm just lying here."

"Really?" She heard his body move, the sheets rustled. She imagined him naked and in bed. She closed her eyes. Ok. She needed to stop doing that right now. "What are you wearing?"

Oh no! They were *not* going to have this conversation. She couldn't handle it. Hell, she couldn't handle *him*. "Christ, Mace, we haven't had one of these conversations in a long time."

"Yeah, but at fourteen they were relatively tame. We're much older now."

"Don't remind me."

"So?"

"So what?"

"What are you wearing?"

"I'm not discussing that with—"

"Are you naked?"

"No!" Dez rolled her eyes. Good god, the man could be persistent. "A tank top and baggy shorts."

"Panties?"

With a throat clear, "No."

He purred. At least that's exactly what it sounded like. Purring. She didn't remember him purring before.

"Did you . . . did you just purr?"

"Yup. I'm thinking about you with no underwear."

"Jesus, Mace. You're killing me."

"Is it making you wet?"

"Mason Llewellyn! We are *not* having this conversation."

"Why?"

"Well, I am hoping to eventually arrest your sister for murder."

"I'm hoping you arrest my sister for murder."

"Oh."

"You're running out of excuses."

"I am not."

"Your nipples hard?"

"Mace!"

"Give me something. I'm dyin' here." Every once in a while, Mace suddenly reminded her he was born and raised in New York when a little bit of an accent reared its ugly head. It usually only happened when he got emotional or, if she remembered her school days correctly, horny . . .

She ground her teeth together. She would *not* have phone sex with a guy she hadn't seen in more than twenty years. Even she wasn't that desperate. "What do you want from me, Mace?"

There went that damn purr again. Deep. Low from his gut. Primal. "Everything."

Dez closed her eyes. *Good answer.* But also the wrong one. She didn't have everything to give. She was a cop. Born a cop if you happened to ask her dad. The one thing in her life that made her truly happy. The one thing she did really well. She couldn't give that up to Mace. She couldn't give that up to anybody.

"You got quiet all of a sudden. What's wrong?"

Dez sighed. "I'm thinking about the price I pay to be me."

Mace chuckled. "What's so funny, Llewellyn?"

"You. You haven't changed one damn bit."

"Are you kidding? I am not the person you used to know."

"No. You're the person I always knew you were."

Dez pulled herself up to a sitting position. "Is that right? And what deep insight do you have about me right now?"

"That's easy. You're thinking you're not about to give up being a cop for me or any man. Aren't you?"

Dez placed the phone on the comforter and scowled at it. She had the almost overwhelming desire to run from the room screaming. She forgot Mace used to do this to her all the time. That he saw what no one else saw. What no one else wanted to see. Sometimes her own family included.

"Pick up the phone, Dez."

She shook her head. *It's not a picture phone, you idiot!*

"I can hear you breathing. So pick up the phone—*now.*"

Dez grabbed the phone and put it to her ear. "How did you . . . when did you . . . ?"

"Come out to dinner with me, Dez."

"No way!" She would not be dating Rasputin anytime soon.

"You either come out here for a nice normal dinner or I come there . . . and who knows what I'll tell you about yourself."

Would that be before or after her dogs rip his arms off? Or she fucks him on the porch. You know . . . whatever.

"This is—"

"Blackmail. Yes. I know. I'm a rich, white male not afraid to use the power of his position." She rolled her eyes, imagining Mace's smile as he spouted that load of crap. "So come out with me anyway. Just dinner. I promise."

"Mace—"

"Come out with me, Dez." His voice actually got lower. How? "Come out with me tonight. Please?"